Lastly, she turned on Forollkin and Kerish. To the young soldier she said: "Yours is a long road, the hard road of sorrow, and you . . ." Looking at Kerish, for the first time she faltered. "Your death is strange and distant and I cannot see it clearly, but for the rest of you there shall be murder. Cursed are the rulers and cursed are the ruled. Cursed is Golden Galkis and cursed are the Godborn!"

"No," cried Lord Izeldon. "No!" He strode the length of the hall until he stood before the priestess of Imarko. "All may come to pass as you prophesy, but in Zeldin the Compassionate there is hope. What is promised will be given, if we ask, if we seek."

The fire of prophesy died from Ka-Metranee's eyes. Her face became gentle, her voice meek.

"You speak of the Promised One?"

"I do."

The High Priestess began to weep. "But who will seek him out? Who will free him from his prison?"

GERALDINE HARRIS has written several books for young adults. She lives in Oxford, England.

ALSO AVAILABLE IN LAUREL-LEAF BOOKS:

SEVEN CITADELS ◆ PART I

PRINCE
OF THE
GODBORN

GERALDINE HARRIS

Published by
Dell Publishing Co., Inc.
1 Dag Hammarskjold Plaza
New York, New York 10017

This work was first published in Great Britain by Macmillan Children's Books.

To Jomsborg and its Reeves

Laurel-Leaf Library ® TM 766734, Dell Publishing Co., Inc.

ISBN: 0-440-95407-X

RL: 6.5

Reprinted by arrangement with Greenwillow Books, a division of William Morrow & Company, Inc.

Printed in the United States of America

August 1987

10 9 8 7 6 5 4 3 2 1

WFH

THE HOUSE OF THE EMPERORS

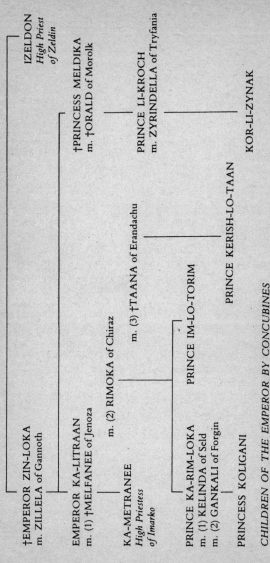

†EMPEROR ZIN-LOKA
m. ZILLELA of Gannoth

IZELDON
High Priest
of Zeldin

EMPEROR KA-LITRAAN
m. (1) †MELFANEE of Jenoza
m. (2) RIMOKA of Chiraz

†PRINCESS MELDIKA
m. †ORALD of Morolk

PRINCE LI-KROCH
m. ZYRINDELLA of Tryfania

KA-METRANEE
High Priestess
of Imarko

m. (3) †TAANA of Erandachu

KOR-LI-ZYNAK

PRINCE IM-LO-TORIM

PRINCE KERISH-LO-TAAN

PRINCE KA-RIM-LOKA
m. (1) KELINDA of Seld
m. (2) GANKALI of Forgin

PRINCESS KOLIGANI

CHILDREN OF THE EMPEROR BY CONCUBINES

1 By †VALDISSA

2 By FOLLEA

3 By †MELZEEN (wife of the Governor of Tryfania)

LORD JERENAC

LORD FOROLLKIN

ZYRINDELLA

Chapter 1

The Book of the Emperors: *Chronicles*

And in the morning of the world, Zeldin took his son by the hand and led him to the summit of a high mountain. As Mikeld-lo-Taan looked down on the wide lands and bright rivers of Galkis, Zeldin said: "All that you behold, from the mountains of the north to the jungles of the south, from the deserts of the east to the seas of the west, shall be a Kingdom to you and to your heirs for ever." Then Mikeld-lo-Taan, first Emperor of Galkis, knelt before his father and swore to build him there a temple.

THE escort of Prince Kerish-lo-Taan halted at the end of a narrow valley. In front of them squatted a shadowy complex of buildings. Lord Forollkin spurred his roan mare through the gates of the Royal Lodge and into the main courtyard. Through the centuries the Lodge had been enlarged until it was almost a palace in itself where the Emperors of Galkis and their families stayed when they came to worship Zeldin on the Holy Mountain. Only one royal standard now flew above the Royal Lodge: the silver Starflower of the Emperor's only nephew, Prince Li-Kroch.

Forollkin drew his sword and struck the bronze gong that hung beside the central doors. Then he waited, shivering under his heavy cloak. After a minute the Keeper of the Royal Lodge, swathed in furs, came down the steps. He bowed just as much as was necessary to the son of a Royal Concubine. Forollkin saluted and announced formally: "His Serene Highness, Prince Kerish-lo-Taan, Third Son of the Emperor Ka-Litraan, may his reign be eternal, demands admittance to the Royal Lodge."

The Keeper bowed again, much lower. "The Lodge

1

would be honoured to receive his Highness, but tomorrow we expect other royal guests for the Presentation ceremony. The High Priest has therefore sent word that the Third Prince is to stay in the temple itself. I believe that his Highness will find Lord Yxin already there."

Masking his annoyance, Forollkin saluted again and rode back to where the soldiers of the escort huddled, stamping and blowing to keep warm. The Prince's litter had been set down, and the purple curtains were half open. The escort were tired. They had been travelling since dawn and all but Forollkin were on foot. Now they had a steep climb ahead of them. Nor would the Prince's temper be improved by lodging with Lord Yxin. Forollkin dismounted and, kneeling by the litter, delivered the High Priest's message to his half-brother.

Kerish-lo-Taan was veiled and hooded for travelling. Only his eyes were visible but they were enough to show his anger.

"Yet I see they can find room for my cousin, the royal idiot."

"Many would think it an honour to be lodged in the temple itself," said Forollkin patiently. "If we leave now, we shall barely reach it by sunset. May I give the order?"

He knew as well as the Prince that they had no choice but he was generous enough not to say so. Kerish sat obstinately silent. Forollkin changed his tactics.

"Highness, our men are cold and hungry and tired; the sooner we reach shelter, any shelter . . ."

Red tinged the Prince's pale cheeks.

"Don't crouch here chattering like a Jenozan monkey then. Give the order!"

Forollkin remounted, grinning to himself. Four soldiers hoisted the litter on to their shoulders and the rest of the escort fell in behind. Kerish-lo-Taan drew the purple curtains. His request that he might ride to the temple on his own fierce, black mare had been refused. This was a court ceremony. The less exalted might ride, or even walk. A Prince of the Godborn must be slowly and tediously carried. Unobserved, Kerish curled up among the soft cushions and was soon lulled into sleep by the rhythmic swaying of the litter.

Forollkin rode ahead, spurring his tired horse. Through clefts of night-black rock the temple road spiralled upwards. It was paved with white marble and flanked with pillars carved with the names and achievements of a hundred generations of High Priests. The air was clear and cold. Turning in his saddle, Forollkin looked down over the great plain of central Galkis. The fading sunlight glinted on the placid waters of the river Gal and the walls of the ancient capital, Golden Galkis, the Queen of Cities.

One of the bearers stumbled, jolting Kerish awake. Forollkin ordered a brief halt and changed the bearers. The escort moved on at a quicker pace. If darkness caught them still on the mountain, they had no torches and the temple road was often dangerously narrow. Within minutes they had crossed the snowline. The cold became more intense and an icy wind billowed the purple curtains. In spite of his furs, Kerish-lo-Taan shivered where he lay.

It was almost nine years since he had travelled this road to his own ceremony of Presentation. A few days before the ceremony, his stepmother Rimoka had smiled at him and said, "Well, slave-girl's son, now we shall see if your mother was as true as she boasted. Woe betide you if you have none of the blood of the Godborn to protect you from the anger of Zeldin."

All through the ceremony Kerish had expected the roof of the temple to split open and Zeldin to strike him down as a nameless imposter. Instead the Presentation had gone smoothly and he had been accepted as a Prince of the Godborn, a true descendant of Zeldin.

Forollkin called out as he sighted the temple of Zeldin. The soldiers, who had been thinking of their destination in terms of warmth and food, found instead beauty to gape at. The star-shaped temple was built in translucent alabaster that changed colour with the light. In bright sun it was golden, in moonlight pale glimmering blue and now, in the last moments of sunset, it blazed crimson.

Kerish and his escort watched until the sun sank below the edge of the world, leaving the temple stark white against the sudden darkness. Forollkin rode forward and

3

hammered on the silver gates. They were swiftly opened by silent, pale-robed priests. Forollkin and his soldiers were relieved of their swords and motioned inside.

The Prince's litter was carried through a long alabaster tunnel and out into a wide, paved courtyard. Kerish at once noticed a blue standard. It was marked with the silver mountain of Tryfania, the second of the Galkian Empire's four great provinces. Forollkin dismounted and planted Kerish's own purple and golden standard in the snow next to Lord Yxin's.

The Prince stepped out of his litter. The soldiers were shown to their quarters and Forollkin's mare and the two pack-horses were led away. Kerish was passably polite to the priest who welcomed them, and asked to be shown to his rooms at once. The priest spoke sympathetically of a tiring journey and led them to a suite of rooms overlooking an inner courtyard. They were small and austerely furnished, but warmed by sweet-smelling fires.

"If there is anything your Highness requires, strike the silver gong by the door. Supper will be brought to you presently." The priest bowed and withdrew.

Kerish began pacing round the small rooms like an animal exploring its cage. Then he flung open the shutters and stood for several minutes gazing across the courtyard. Forollkin discarded his heavy travelling cloak. Kerish spoke, his breath clouding the frosty air.

"I wonder where Lord Yxin is lodged? Do you think over the courtyard there, or. . . ?"

"I think your death will catch you sooner than it should, if you lean out of windows on a night like this. Come to the fire."

Kerish slammed the shutters and crossed to the hearth.

"If I'd known we'd be staying here instead of the Lodge, I'd have brought servants but. . . ."

"As it is, I'll wait on you," finished Forollkin, "unless you'd prefer a deft-handed novice."

"Oh no."

He sounded as if he was smiling.

"Then give me your cloak."

Kerish took off the cloak and unwound his veil and

4

hood. Then he perched on a stool while Forollkin tugged off his leather boots.

There was little in the young men's looks to indicate their close kinship. Forollkin was tall, big-boned and sturdy. A pleasant rather than handsome face was notable only for its grey, gold-flecked eyes. Forollkin's long, brown hair was neatly cut, his uniform immaculate. His sun-darkened skin spoke of the active life of a soldier as surely as his brother's pallor hinted at the closed world of the Inner Palace.

Kerish-lo-Taan was small, fine-boned and slender. His hair was black, marred by the broad silver streak that was an inheritance from his foreign mother. His face might have been the ivory mask of an idol, perfectly carved, yet inexpressive. Inexpressive until you looked into the eyes. For they were the eyes of the Royal House of Galkis, the eyes of Zeldin, the eyes of the Godborn. The irises were deep violet flecked with gold, the pupils blacker than midnight. Strange, unfathomable eyes. Even Forollkin never looked straight into them if he could avoid it.

The priest returned with three novices deputed to wait on the Prince. A frugal supper was laid on a table near the fire. There was white cheese and bread, fruit from the mountain vineyards and hot, spiced wine. When they were alone again Kerish and Forollkin sat down opposite each other, the length of the table between them. The Prince toyed with some fruit and drank two cups of wine. Forollkin watched his half-brother warily. The Prince was restless, his cheeks flushed, his eyes brighter than ever. Probably signs of the temper he had been nourishing for the past three days.

"The fruit is sour!" said Kerish and tossed his portion into the fire.

Forollkin watched as it withered and burned and then answered calmly, "The cheese has a fine, strong flavour and the bread is good."

"Coarse cheese is hardly fit for princes."

"No, but this is a temple not a palace."

"At Hildimarn my brother's temple serves finer food than any palace."

5

"True, but then everyone knows where Prince Im-lo-Torim's devotion lies."

For a moment Forollkin thought he had provoked his brother into real anger but suddenly Kerish started to laugh.

"Yes, every time I see him his belt is an inch wider and you'd still think he couldn't have room for half of what he eats ... but Forollkin ..." He reached across the table to grip the young soldier's wrist, "you mustn't say things like that to anyone but me. Do you promise?"

"I promise, and I know I can trust you."

There was a rap on the door.

"Enter," called the Prince, releasing Forollkin's wrist. The priest and his novices came in to clear the table.

"I trust your Highness ate well. Have you any wish that I may grant?"

"I thank you, nothing," answered Kerish.

"His Holiness will receive you in the morning. May you have quiet sleep," said the priest, and withdrew with his novices after their offers of service were rejected.

Forollkin helped his half-brother to undress and saw him huddled beneath a fur coverlet. Then he stoked up the fire and lay down on the couch in the outer room. Forollkin sank into a shallow sleep almost at once but Kerish lay awake far into the watches of the night, listening to the ringing of silver wind chimes and the faint, distant chanting of the priests.

The Prince slept long past the dawn bell. At nine, Forollkin strode into the bedroom and opened the shutters. The pale morning sunlight streaked across the Prince's face. He blinked and opened his eyes. The figure of Forollkin was black against the window.

"It's past the third bell and you've lost half a fine morning."

"Sleep is gain, not loss," said Kerish, sitting up and stretching. "You have it too easily to prize it, and enjoy it too quietly."

"Did you dream again?" asked Forollkin sharply.

Kerish nodded as he reluctantly disentangled himself from the fur coverlet.

"Yes, but it wasn't so bad this time. There was a door I had to open but I had no key. I beat against it till I woke." He looked at his hands as if he expected to see real bruises.

"Forget it now," said Forollkin and held out a bowl of scented water.

"I think I should talk to Lord Izeldon."

"Not, I hope, till you've washed, dressed and eaten."

Kerish washed, while Forollkin fetched him an armful of clothes, and then dressed hurriedly in high boots and a long tunic of purple, embroidered in gold. He threaded a comb through his tangled hair and turned to Forollkin.

"Well?"

From birth to death the Godborn were forbidden to look at their own reflections. Only in the Book of Secrets was a reason given but there were no mirrors in the palaces or temples of Galkis.

"Well?" asked Kerish eagerly. "Do you think Lord Yxin will be jealous?"

"Of your clothes or your face?" asked Forollkin, laughing.

"Is nothing out of place?" said Kerish coldly.

Forollkin smoothed a stray lock of hair. "Nothing. Now I've left you some breakfast, if you just . . ."

"I don't eat leavings," snapped Kerish, and tossing a fleece cloak over his shoulder he strode out of the room.

Swearing under his breath, Forollkin followed.

Round a snow-strewn courtyard, overlooked by a hanging gallery, the sound of whipcracks echoed. Impervious to the thin air and icy cold, Lord Yxin and three of his retinue were playing with the long, hide whips they had brought from the north. Their target was a battered goblet placed on a disused altar some twelve feet away. The purpose of the game was to coil the lengths of hide around the goblet and to drag it back to the players' feet. The four young men stood in a line, feet wide apart, their whips coiled in their right hands. Yxin gave a high, clear whistle and four lengths of sharp-edged hide uncoiled with lethal speed. A flick of the wrist and the prize was jerked to Lord Yxin's feet.

"Well played, my Lord," cried one of his attendants, smiling nervously. Yxin carefully unwound the lengths of hide and kicked the goblet away.

"A child could do as much."

"In far Tryfarn perhaps, my Lord," said another of the attendants, "but here in the south they can no more handle a whip than ride the wind."

Lord Yxin glanced up as two cloaked figures entered the gallery.

"Then let us show them how it is done," murmured Yxin. "Kanix, have you a coin?" He turned to his third attendant, who shivered suddenly.

"No, my Lord."

"But I have," announced one of the others. He handed his master a star-shaped golden coin with the Emperor's name on one side and the symbol of Tryfania on the other.

"Thank you, Iroc. Now, Kanix, go and stand beside the altar and hold up the coin."

Kanix walked twelve feet away and, stretching out his arm, held the coil with the very tips of his fingers. Yxin, keeping his eye on the gleaming coin, slowly raised his right arm above his head, then with great force he brought it down. The whip snaked through the air, missed the coin by a fraction and hit the ground with a tremendous crack.

"Oh, very close, my Lord," mouthed Iroc.

"Kanix," snapped his master, "stop shaking!"

Frowning, Lord Yxin drew back the lengths of hide. He raised his arm and again the whip uncoiled with the weight of his body behind it. This time it knocked the coin from Kanix' hand and sliced into his fingers.

"Oh, well hit, my Lord!" cried Iroc.

"Well hit!" echoed the other.

Kanix stared at the first drops of his blood staining the snow.

Lord Yxin smiled and, looking up, seemed to be aware for the first time of the two young men in the gallery.

"Why Prince Kerish and Forollkin, too, welcome to the House of Zeldin."

Yxin was two years older than Kerish but, as the son of a mere Lord Governor of Tryfania, he was far from his equal in rank. Nevertheless, with only his servants watching, Yxin did not trouble to bow. Kerish and Forollkin came down a flight of steps into the courtyard.

"Thank you for your greeting, Yxin, but the High Priest has already welcomed us to the House of Zeldin the Gentle."

"By message only, I believe. The High Priest has not stirred from the sanctuary for the past two days, though when I arrived he came to the gate to meet me."

"No doubt because you have not had the honour to lodge here before," returned Kerish, icily polite.

During this exchange, Forollkin, white-faced with controlled anger, had walked over to Kanix. He cleaned the young man's wounded hand with snow and bound it with his own sash.

Yxin turned towards him. "I've heard that you're a fair hand with the whip yourself, Forollkin. What do you think of our game?"

Kerish tensed but Forollkin answered calmly, "I think, my Lord, that you should take more care. Broken toys are of no use to anyone."

"But what pleasure can there be in a game that has no element of danger?" demanded Yxin.

Forollkin paced towards him. "Since you have a taste for dangerous games, try playing an equal one for a change. Fight me with your whip."

"I might use my whip on the son of a concubine," said Yxin, "but I'd hardly fight one as an equal."

Kerish wrenched Yxin round to face him. "Then fight with me, my Lord of Tryfania. Or do you object to fighting one higher than yourself too?"

Yxin smiled. "I would be honoured to fight with your Highness. Pray take my whip since you have none."

He bowed and walked off to test the whips of his attendants.

Kerish was left staring at the whip pressed into his hand. The ebony handle was carved like a snake. From the serpent's jaws trailed twelve feet of weathered hide, capable of slashing through a man's leg, straight to the bone.

Forollkin took his half-brother by the shoulders. "Kerish, you can't face Yxin with a whip. You hardly know how to use one on a horse, let alone . . . For Zeldin's sake tell him you've changed your mind."

Kerish blazed at him. "Withdraw a challenge and be marked as a coward! You don't know me!"

"Oh, but I do," thought Forollkin, "and you are going to be hurt."

He tried again. "Listen, if you can waste a few minutes arguing the terms of the fight, I'll fetch a priest to stop . . ."

Kerish interrupted. "He offered you an insult. Do you think I could let him do that unchallenged?"

Forollkin had no answer.

Chapter 2

The Book of the Emperors: *Wisdom*
*To be defeated in an equal combat carries no shame. But a
victor who scorns his opponent or a loser who speaks mal-
iciously of a victor, these are not worthy to be called children of
Zeldin. For a man must face defeat many times in the span of
his years and if his defeats are without bitterness, in death he
shall have victory.*

Yxin had chosen a whip.

"Are you ready, Highness?"

Kerish threw off his heavy cloak and nodded. Iroc
stepped between the two young men.

"Royal rules, my Lords, no striking at the face."

Forollkin whispered, "Watch his hands and keep
moving. Zeldin be with you." He squeezed his brother's
shoulder and stepped back.

"Are you ready, my Lords, both in body and mind?"
asked Iroc formally. "Then in the name of the Emperor
fight justly and remember the mercy of Zeldin."

He signalled for the fight to begin.

Yxin was both taller and heavier than Kerish but he
moved as swiftly as a hunting cat. Keeping just out of
range they circled each other, making a great show of
cracking the long whips. Nervously, Kerish attacked first.
Keeping his glance on Yxin's tensed hand, the Prince
darted forward and lashed out wildly. Yxin danced away
and the lethal coils struck the ground several feet from
where he now stood. Kerish flung himself back as Yxin
returned the stroke, and escaped by inches.

Again they circled each other, watching for the slightest
lapse in concentration. Then Yxin sprang, sweeping his
whip sideways, to knock the Prince off his feet. It was a

dangerous stroke that meant getting very close to his opponent. Kerish saw the thin line of agony sweeping towards him. He wavered for a second and then stumbled backwards and out of reach. Yxin laughed and darted towards the Prince swinging his black-handled whip from side to side. No one noticed a tall, silver-haired man enter the gallery.

Forollkin winced as Yxin lashed out again, aiming at the Prince's hands. Kerish avoided that blow and the next, but he was slowly forced to retreat till his back was against the courtyard wall. Forollkin knew that Yxin would not dare to kill the Prince but in a formal combat he could wound or even maim, without reproach. Yxin and Kerish attacked at the same moment. Their whips met and tangled in mid air, the force of the impact jarring them both. Yxin pulled his whip free first and sliced a blow at the Prince's right side. Kerish dodged but not quickly enough.

The toughened hide tore through the Prince's thick sleeve and bit into his skin. As Yxin swiftly drew back the whip along the line of the wound Kerish gasped with pain. Forollkin began to run towards them but found Iroc barring his way. Kerish still held the whip but his right arm hung limp. With a flick of his wrist Yxin sent the thin, cruel lengths coiling around Kerish's legs. Before the Prince could move he was bound from thighs to ankles in loops of hide. With one vicious tug Yxin pulled the coils tight and dragged Kerish to the ground. The Prince rolled helplessly in the snow. Yxin loosed the handle of the whip and began to laugh.

"Oh well fought, my Lord, most well fought!" cried Iroc.

"Your mercy does you credit, my Lord," murmured the second attendant.

Kanix stood silent, nursing his wounded hand.

Yxin picked up his own whip from where Kerish had dropped it and coiled it round and round his hand.

"It would be ignoble," began Yxin, "to take advantage of the Prince's delicacy . . ."

"Delicacy, Yxin," interrupted a gentle voice, "is not necessarily a fault."

Yxin spun round and his attendants knelt as Lord Izeldon came down into the courtyard.

Still speaking quietly, the High Priest of Zeldin asked what had taken place.

"A game, your Holiness," said Yxin, suddenly subdued.

"A game?" queried Izeldon. "There is blood on the snow."

"Prince Kerish-lo-Taan challenged his Lordship," put in Iroc but the High Priest still looked only at Yxin.

"And your servant. Was he challenged too?"

"An accident," muttered Yxin.

"I see," murmured the High Priest. "A challenge you could not in honour refuse and an accident you could not avoid. My child, you must thank Zeldin for his mercies to you; a whole day spent in his sanctuary would scarcely suffice. And, Yxin . . . on your knees."

He beckoned to one of the priests who attended him. "Escort his Lordship to the Inner Sanctuary, and see that his servant is tended."

With a sulky bow of obedience Lord Yxin left the court-yard with his attendants.

Forollkin had already rushed to where his brother lay. Kerish was struggling to free himself from the coils of the whip. Forollkin slipped an arm under his brother's shoulder and tugged at the coils with his free hand. Through the torn leather of the Prince's sleeve gaped a slash the width of his arm. Kerish pushed his brother away and struggled to his feet. He found the handle of the whip and freed himself from its harsh embrace. Forollkin gently took hold of Kerish's arm and examined it.

"The cut is deep, but at least it's clean."

Sick with unassuaged anger, Kerish covered the wound with his hand and turned away muttering, "Leave it alone."

Forollkin, his sympathy rejected, said briskly, "The Healing Priests will soon mend it. I'll take you."

Kerish shook his head.

"Now come on, you can't stand shivering here . . ."
Forollkin stopped himself and put an arm around his half-

brother's good shoulder.

"Kerish, don't grieve over the foredoomed. You couldn't hope to beat Yxin. He was born with a whip in his hand. Next time remember to strike more to the right when . . ."

Kerish span round shouting, "Why can't you leave me alone!" and swung the recovered whip at Forollkin's face.

Totally surprised, Forollkin made no attempt to ward off the blow. The hide met the flesh of his right cheek with a dull hiss. Kerish lowered the whip and stared. Blood welled from a deep disfiguring cut. For a moment everything was still, then Forollkin slowly raised a hand to his cheek. Kerish made a choking sound in his throat, turned violently away and found himself staring into the eyes of the High Priest of Zeldin.

Lord Izeldon held out his hand. "Kerish-lo-Taan, give that to me."

Kerish handed the whip to him. Then, finding the questioning look in those eyes unbearable, he fled blindly out of the courtyard.

Izeldon called gently after him but he did not hear.

Forollkin fumbled for his sash, forgetting that he had given it to Kanix. The High Priest walked towards him.

"Forollkin, let me see the hurt."

The young soldier tried to wrench himself out of his daze of shock.

"If your Holiness will allow, I'll go to the healers and have this tended. It's hardly more than a scratch."

His cheek burned as he spoke.

"Then perhaps my meagre talent as a healer will suffice," said Izeldon, with the faintest glimmer of a smile.

Forollkin had never been to the High Priest's quarters before and he marvelled at their simplicity. Smooth alabaster walls, broken by high, shuttered windows, enclosed a small room. No fire warmed the sparsely-furnished chamber, no figured hangings softened its austerity, but on a window-sill stood a bowl of orchids from the Emperor's garden. Forollkin, sitting on a hard bench trying to forget the pain in his cheek, noted all this.

Then Izeldon was beside him carrying a silver bowl full of heated water, a soft white cloth and a handful of herbs. One by one he dropped the herbs into the bowl, speaking their names aloud. Dipping the cloth in the scented water, Izeldon gently bathed Forollkin's cheek. Lastly he pressed his fingertips against the wound and gradually Forollkin felt his cheek grow numb.

The High Priest took his hand away but he continued to study his great-nephew's face.

"Will there be a scar, my Lord?"

Izeldon smiled. "A faint one. Not enough to deter the ladies of Galkis. Has the Prince ever struck you before?"

"No," said Forollkin untruthfully.

Izeldon sat down on the far end of the bench. "There is no need to protect your brother from *me*."

Forollkin was forced to look into the High Priest's eyes, purple, golden and black, the eyes of the Godborn.

"It's just that he's childish," stammered the young soldier, "and quick tempered, but he doesn't mean to hurt."

The High Priest nodded. "You are not compelled to stay with him. What stitches you to your brother's side?"

"My Lord, you heard Yxin call him delicate and you saw he couldn't defend himself. Kerish is clever, of course, but it will take more than that to help him against . . ."

"Against what?"

Forollkin struggled to explain without speaking treason of the Godborn.

"Because he is the Emperor's best-loved son there are enemies even in the Royal Household who might try to hurt him."

"Or murder him," said the High Priest starkly. "Oh, I hear what is whispered behind the veils of the Inner Palace even here, on the Holy Mountain, and I remember his mother and how much she was hated."

Izeldon got up and walked to the window. "So you have protected Kerish, but soon he will be of age. What then? He will be sent to govern some great city and you have your own life. You are born of different worlds; do you wish to stay with him always?"

"Different worlds, yes," thought Forollkin, "mine bright sunlight, action and danger and nothing I can't understand by the touch of my two hands, but his . . ." He said aloud: "I will stay as long as he needs me."

"That is generous," said Izeldon. "And do you never need your brother's help?"

"Kerish's?" Forollkin laughed. "I'd as soon ask the wind."

"Kerish-lo-Taan has all the gifts of the Godborn," murmured the High Priest.

"But I have not," answered Forollkin, "and I don't understand them."

Izeldon smiled tiredly. "Forgive my questions, they are not without purpose. But have you ever told your brother that you love him?"

Any answer that Forollkin might have made was drowned by the braying of trumpets. The High Priest listened for a moment.

"Lord Jerenac, I think. Forollkin, go down to the main gate and greet him for me. I must look for Kerish."

When the young man had left, Izeldon knelt for a moment in prayer, the mask of serenity stripped from his face.

Lord Jerenac handed his great, silver-hilted sword to the priests, and dismounted. Born of a Royal Concubine he was, at thirty-eight, the oldest of the Emperor's children. A tall man, lean and hard, his black mane of hair was already streaked with iron grey. He was carelessly dressed in shabby leather and a cloak of shaggy fur, but the heavy gold and lapis armlets, which he wore with so little grace, could have bought a town. One of Jerenac's men planted in the snow the lilac and silver banner of the Governor of Jenoza and Lord Commander of the armies of Galkis.

Jerenac, impatient to have the formal welcome over, was to his pleasure greeted by Forollkin rather than some soft-spoken priest. The Lord Commander approved of his half-brother, a brave, neat, practical young man, skilled in the arts of war. They were the only arts Jerenac chose to pursue. He noticed the clotted scar on Forollkin's cheek and pointed to it. Forollkin abandoned the High Priest's welcome as the Lord Commander clearly was not listening.

"An accident, Sir," said Forollkin stiffly, "with a whip."

"The Third Prince here?"

"Yes, Sir, and Lord Yxin."

Jerenac grunted.

"There is food and wine laid out for you, my Lord," said Forollkin, "if you will come with me."

Lord Jerenac dismissed his soldiers and waved away the priests who would have attended him.

In a triangular room in one of the points of the star, food and wine were spread for the Lord Commander. Tossing his cloak into a corner, Jerenac slumped down and attacked the meal. Forollkin stood as his commander devoured cheese, bread and fruit.

"No meat," grunted Jerenac, tearing the skin off a girt.

"Not in a temple, Sir!" exclaimed Forollkin.

Jerenac spat out a pip. "Priests of Zeldin, afraid of the taste of blood."

"They will not shed blood, my Lord."

Taciturn in public, Jerenac could speak well enough when he chose.

"Soon they must decide to sanction war, or see the Dark Goddess squat in the ruins of their temples."

Forollkin handed a cup of wine to his commander.

"There is news, Sir?"

Jerenac looked into the earnest grey eyes of his half-brother and nodded.

"Speak no word of this, not even to Kerish-lo-Taan. The Five Kingdoms have sworn an alliance in the name of the Dark Goddess."

The Lord Commander governed Jenoza, the Empire's southernmost province. Its capital was the great, white-walled city of Viroc on the banks of the river Jenze, but beyond Viroc, beyond the river, lay Oraz, easternmost of the Five Kingdoms. For centuries the rulers of the Five Kingdoms had savaged each other in countless petty wars. Though they were of one race and worshipped the same goddess, there had never been peace between the kingdoms. But if a formal alliance had been signed . . . Forallkin knew that the men of the Five Kingdoms could as soon stop breathing as fighting.

"You think they will turn on us?"

"Where else?" demanded Jerenac. "The desert of Kolg and the desolation of Zarn lie to the west and south of them. The sea is to the north and they are not great seafarers, though they have the friendship of the fleet of Fangmere. If they would fight anyone but each other they must come east."

"We have defeated them before."

"We have defeated the Princes of Oraz, and sometimes of Mintaz but never a combined army of the Five Kingdoms."

"Then we must garrison the border, fortify the river."

Jerenac smiled for the first time.

"I have not ridden hundreds of miles solely to attend a foolish ceremony. I came to ask the Emperor for men and gold. If need be, men from the north."

"But the brigands of Fangmere!" protested Forollkin. "If you take men from the north, then Hildimarn . . ."

"May be frightened into disgorging some of its temple treasures to pay for my armies."

Lord Jerenac swallowed the red wine in one gulp and his young half-brother refilled the cup.

"Well now, Forollkin," said the Lord Commander, leaning back in his chair. "Night is gathering. Where will you be? North harrying the brigands? South with me? Or here at your pale Prince's side?"

The wound on Forollkin's cheek was beginning to ache again.

"The Prince will soon be of age," he said.

"And you are not his keeper," growled Jerenac, "though he may need one. Forollkin, I have always thought well of you. You know one end of a sword from another which is more than can be said for most of our royal kin. You fought boldly against the men of Fangmere, though that was only skirmishing. In the south, in Viroc, in Jenoza, I have need of young warriors like you. Then, you are of

18

royal blood, my blood. It is fitting that you should command and I have no son."

Jerenac stood up. "When I ride south, Forollkin, ride with me, as my chief Captain. Serve me well and you may take my place as Lord Commander when my stars darken. But mind, you have my support only if you serve *me*, and *me* alone, and cease to cling to the Third Prince or any of our royal kin. Well, boy?"

This of course was what he had always wanted, or at least what he had told himself he wanted. It was true: nothing bound him to Kerish, he had no obligation. Forollkin touched the scar on his cheek. No obligation at all, and yet . . . clearly he heard the High Priest's question: "Have you ever told your brother you love him?" and his own unspoken answer. Kerish's mother had died before her twentieth birthday.

"Well, boy?"

"My, my Lord," Forollkin stammered, "may I give you my answer tomorrow after the ceremony?"

Jerenac scowled. "You may, but I did not think to hear you hesitate. Pause to think in battle and you'll find a sword in your guts."

"I know it," said Forollkin.

Kerish-lo-Taan ran blindly though the empty and echoing chambers of the Inner Temple. It was absurd to cry, it made him even more angry. Tears scalded his cheeks and he shook with rage against himself.

"I am a man," thought Kerish. "I am a man. I won't cry. I won't! I'll go back and apologize to Forollkin. I'll tell him I'm sorry, though I'm not. He treats me like a child. I'm not sorry."

Kerish tripped on a step and fell heavily, jarring his wounded shoulder. The pain sobered him and his gasping breath quietened.

He sat up slowly and looked around him. Unnoticing, he had entered the central hall of the temple, a vast, coldly beautiful room of palest alabaster, inlaid with marvellous designs in silver and cirge. The room was empty and quiet but Kerish gasped again as he looked up for he had fallen at the very feet of the Gentle God. Above him towered an ancient stone statue of Zeldin, his arms spread in blessing, his face serene and smiling. It was a young face and Kerish had always found that strange. His life was ordered by so many old people but the god they worshipped was eternally young. The features of Zeldin might have been modelled on his father but there was no such serenity in the man who hid in the Palace gardens and let the Empire rot. They might have belonged to his brothers if their faces had not been overlaid by the marks of greed and idleness, or to himself if . . . Kerish jerked away from the thought.

His sandalled feet slapping against the marble floor, Lord Izeldon entered the hall. He looked into the face of his master and returned the smile of the Gentle God.

"My dear child, much as it pleases me to see you at your devotions, your wound should be tended."

Kerish jumped up. "My Lord?"

Izeldon came closer to him. "You are bleeding, child."

"Don't call me child," snapped Kerish.

"Forgive me," said the High Priest gently. "It is a fault of old age. What would you like me to call you? Highness? Nephew?"

"Just Kerish. It is my name."

"I understand," murmured Izeldon. "I remember how it irked me once to be known only as the Emperor's son, the Emperor's brother, the Emperor's uncle . . ."

Kerish looked at the High Priest curiously. They had only met before on very formal occasions and he was not sure if he was being teased.

"I didn't mean to be insolent."

"I know that my dear chi . . . my dear Kerish, but try to think before you speak or your own words will plague you all your life long."

"Yes, your Holiness," agreed Kerish meekly.

"Now come with me and I will tend your arm. The blood of the Godborn is too precious to waste."

Like Forollkin, Kerish had never been in the High Priest's apartments before. He was drawn at once to the bowl of orchids and touched their delicate petals.

"I see you are your father's son," said Izeldon, returning

with water and herbs.

"I love all beautiful things," said Kerish.

"That is good," answered the High Priest. "But don't imagine that beauty is always easily recognized. Give me your arm."

Kerish winced as Izeldon's gentle fingers probed the slash in his arm.

"My Lord," began Kerish hesitantly, "you haven't spoken about what I did."

Izeldon began to bathe the Prince's arm.

"No, that is a matter between you and Forollkin."

"And you don't want to punish me?"

"You are punishing yourself quite adequately."

"It's just that he makes me angry, treating me like a child. He never . . . but I shall apologize, I promise."

"Thank you, Kerish."

Izeldon carefully bandaged his great-nephew's arm.

"My Lord," said Kerish suddenly, "would you be angry if I asked you a question?"

"I think it very unlikely," murmured the High Priest. "It is one of my tasks to stir people into asking questions."

"The Book of the Emperors tells us that we are divine, the descendants of the Gentle God." Kerish spoke hurriedly, staring straight ahead. "And that Zeldin can accomplish anything; rend the earth, scatter the stars, hold the seas in the palm of his hand . . . yet it is *us* that he loves. Holiness, I cannot see why! My father, my brothers, myself, we are *not* all good or all wise. How can we be the children of a god and why should we rule Galkis?"

Izeldon sat down on the window-sill beside Kerish, his hands folded in his lap. He did not answer immediately.

"Are you angry, my Lord?" asked Kerish.

"No. I am considering your questions and I think them good ones, though I believe there is one you have left out. If we are false, may our god not be a mockery also?"

The High Priest saw Kerish flinch but he went on placidly. "I sometimes think that faith is like climbing a stair in total darkness. If you are fortunate you may get just one flash of light to show you where you are going . . . but to your questions.

"Remember, Kerish, though our Forefather was Zeldin himself, our Foremother, our Lady Imarko, was human and died a human death. We were, and are, half human. Zeldin did not make us gods. He gave us a choice: to act like beasts, like men, or like gods. Choice is our glory and our curse and for many generations we have chosen basely.

"As for the powers of the Godborn, I am the last to have been fully trained in their use. Your father forbade me to teach any of his children, and I begin to think there was wisdom in that. We have forgotten that the heart of our strength was to see Zeldin in all men. Now we hold ourselves apart and the Empire crumbles with our lost faith and Jerenac howls for swords to meet violence with greater violence."

"Someone once told me," said Kerish, "that you almost became a soldier instead of a priest."

"That is true. Once my ambition was to be Lord Commander of Galkis." Izeldon smiled in self-mockery. "It was not the will of Zeldin but I have fought to keep Galkis to the way of the Godborn. I have fought and I have lost each battle."

Kerish shifted uncomfortably as he began to sense the anger hidden behind the High Priest's serenity.

"Your father will not listen to my counsels and avenges your mother's death on us all. Your brothers tread their own paths to destruction. Jerenac speaks only of blood and Zyrindella weaves her web of treachery. Our prophets knew it long ago: *When there is hate in the eyes of the Godborn, the Empire will drown in its own blood and the glory of Galkis fade and die.* You are wondering why I am telling you all this. If I had only despair to offer I would remain silent. Kerish, do you remember the one comfort that our prophets give us?"

Kerish nodded. He had been made to recite the passage many times by his tutors. *Let the Seven Gates be opened and the prison broken. For the one who is imprisoned beyond the Seventh Gate shall be a Saviour to restore the peace of Zeldin to the children of Galkis.*

"I am the carrier of that hope," said Izeldon softly, "but I have no heir. I must tell you, Kerish, that I invited you and

Forollkin and Yxin to the temple itself so that I might observe you and make a choice."

Kerish looked down at the orchids. "And I have already failed you."

"I have not made my decision yet," answered Izeldon.

"But what . . ." Kerish was silenced by a gesture.

"No more questions now, Kerish. We must go down to the gate. Three more guests wait at Zeldin's door."

When Prince Li-Kroch and his wife and son entered the temple the High Priest and Kerish-lo-Taan stood waiting for them. A fourth standard was planted in the snow and three elaborate litters set down on the marble paving. The scented curtains of the first litter were drawn back and the Princess Zyrindella slithered out. Her slender form was swathed in glossy furs but beneath her shadowy veil black and golden eyes blazed in a cold, white face.

"In the name of Zeldin the Gentle and of Imarko his queen, you are welcome, Lady," pronounced the High Priest.

Zyrindella curtsied deeply to Izeldon and perfunctorily to Kerish-lo-Taan.

"Your Holiness is most gracious." She smiled, showing her sharp, white teeth.

The High Priest turned to the small figure behind her.

"And to you, my son, a special welcome, for this is your festival."

The child stared at him open-mouthed. Wrapped in furs, all that could be seen of Lord Kor-li-Zynak was a thin, sallow face, and huge, frightened eyes, black-ringed with tiredness. Zyrindella turned and struck him lightly on the cheek.

"Thank his Holiness!"

Kor-li-Zynak put his face in his hands and began to cry.

Before Zyrindella could speak again, the High Priest murmured, "Poor child, he is tired from his journey and must rest. A room has been prepared where he may remain in seclusion until the ceremony."

"And I will be with him." Zyrindella's hands closed on the boy's thin shoulders.

"Of course."

It was customary, or the High Priest's reply would have been different.

Suddenly from behind the closed curtains of the third litter came a high-pitched laugh. Kerish winced. For he knew the sound.

Zyrindella turned round and tugged open the curtains, tearing the thin silk.

Among the cushions huddled Prince Li-Kroch. In his hands hung a string of black pearls which he had been counting over and over again. Zyrindella snatched the necklace.

"I have searched for that these past five days and beaten my handmaid for losing it."

"Black," muttered Prince Li-Kroch, "black eyes with all the brightness burned away."

He laughed again, a high jarring sound.

Kerish might have been sorry for Zyrindella if he hadn't known that the marriage was of her own choice. Daughter of the Emperor by the Governor of Tryfania's wife, she had bound herself to the Emperor's only nephew so that no one could dispute her place among the Godborn. If the rumours of the Inner Palace were to be believed, she did not lack for saner company.

Lord Izeldon crossed to the litter and gave his hand to help Li-Kroch out.

"Welcome, Highness," he said, "to the House of Peace."

Li-Kroch smiled sweetly at him and began solemnly, "I give you thanks, my Lord ... my Lord..." His voice trailed away and the mad Prince wandered across the snow to where the royal standards rippled. He was followed by two hard-faced servants, his constant shadows. Among the cushions of the Prince's litter lay the small corpse of a gold-collared monkey. Li-Kroch loved animals but his pets seldom survived his caresses for long.

Zyrindella finished winding the black pearls around her throat and said, "If my husband troubles you, give him this."

She handed the High Priest a phial. He knew from the

sickly smell that it was zigul. One sip would send the mad Prince into a dull trance in which he would obey his keepers without thought.

"I trust in Zeldin that it will not be needed," murmured the High Priest.

"Ah, your Holiness is gentle-hearted, but remember he is cunning. Last moon he escaped from the Inner Palace and we found him wandering the streets of Galkis with stray dogs at his heels!"

Zyrindella laughed.

"I will conduct you to your chamber," said the High Priest, his face impassive. "Kerish, will you take your cousin to the pavilion that overlooks the bronze courtyard. You know the way?"

"Yes, your Holiness."

To Kerish's surprise, Li-Kroch recognized his voice and came to him smiling.

"Kerish, sweet Kerish, purple and gold, silver and black."

He embraced his young cousin, kissing him on the forehead. Kerish shuddered but did not move. The mad Prince was like a travesty of himself. They shared the same, coldly beautiful features but Li-Kroch's chalk white face was marred by shadows. His eyes were the same violet and gold, but sometimes glassily vacant, sometimes gleaming and vicious. The Prince's long, black hair hung tangled on his shoulders. His rich robes and furs trailed unnoticed on the ground and his hands were scarred.

Kerish smiled nervously. "Cousin, will you come with me?"

"What, to walk in the Emperor's garden?" asked Li-Kroch. "There are flowers in your father's garden, red and gaping like wounds. I saw one eat a bird once."

"We'll go there another day," said Kerish.

Reluctantly he took his cousin's arm and guided him along. The two servants followed behind at a discreet distance. Prince Li-Kroch chattered incessantly about the flowers and animals of the Emperor's garden as they passed down long alabaster corridors and through snow-drifted courtyards. Kerish hardly listened. His legs were stiffened with bruises and every step hurt.

"There are pools of green water deep enough to drown in and lilies scarlet and golden, but the birds cry under my window at night. I set traps but they're too cunning. They laugh and throw my words back at me. Birds with beaks like scimitars and feathers the colour of blood, bright, bright. But you'll see, one night I'll catch them and get my hands around their necks . . ."

Li-Kroch laughed and the sound echoed wildly around the courtyard that they were crossing. Suddenly the Prince's laughter turned to a cry of delight and he knelt in the snow.

"Look, look, beautiful crimson flowers growing for me."

"Come away, cousin," said Kerish. "They're only bloodstains on the snow."

Li-Kroch looked up, his eyes shining. "Blood flowers growing for me."

Kerish took his arm. "Come, cousin, please."

Li-Kroch snarled at him. "No, you shan't take my flowers away," and turning his head he bit into the Prince's hand. Kerish cried out, more in shock than pain.

His cousin, one drop of blood quivering on his lips, sprang at him. In moments the two servants had caught up with them and seizing Li-Kroch they threw him back. One helped Kerish to his feet while the other drew out a thin rope. He held it for the mad Prince to see. The animal fury died and Li-Kroch cowered in the snow.

"Highness," said one of the men, "we'd best tie him. He's not to be trusted."

Li-Kroch heard and understood. He held out his hands in terror to Kerish. "Cousin, sweet cousin, you won't let them tie me? Then the birds can get to me."

The man with the rope advanced. Li-Kroch huddled against the wall muttering, "Sharp, sharp, sharp."

"No," ordered Kerish, "leave him free."

"But your Highness . . ."

"Let him alone. Come, cousin."

Kerish held out a hand on which the Prince's teeth marks

were still visible. Smiling, Li-Kroch took it and they went on together.

On one side of a courtyard lined with panels of white bronze stood a low pavilion. Inside was a dark room, richly furnished and hung with figured silks, musty with age. It was the apartment kept for the Emperor himself when he came to the temple; unused in sixteen years. Li-Kroch at once knelt by the smouldering fire. One of his servants stood close behind him in case he burned his hands trying to pick scarlet flowers.

"Goodbye, cousin," said Kerish, "I will see you at moon-rise."

"The birds," answered Li-Kroch, "the bright birds . . . they can't get in?"

Kerish knew better than to argue this time.

"Look, the shutters are closed, a speck of dust could not enter, let alone a bird."

It was true. Once the door was barred nothing would get in, or out. Li-Kroch smiled and his face seemed younger than Kerish's, in spite of the twelve years between them. Kerish turned to the Prince's keepers.

"Be gentle with him."

He left, nursing his bitten hand. Aching all over now he made his way back, through a maze of passages, to his own quarters and found them empty. Relieved at not having to face Forollkin yet, Kerish tugged off his boots and flung himself down on the bed. He slept almost immediately and was not disturbed by the arrival of two other members of his family.

To the sound of silver trumpets, and followed by a retinue of priests and priestesses, two splendid palanquins were carried into the central court. Already descending from the first was the Emperor's second son, Prince Im-lo-Torim, priestly governor of the sacred city of Hildimarn. The second, tightly curtained litter contained the Emperor's eldest daughter, the Princess Ka-Metranee, virgin High Priestess of Imarko.

Wearily, Izeldon welcomed his great-nephew who

would one day succeed him as High Priest of Zeldin. Prince Im-lo-Torim prostrated himself in ceremonial humility and carefully shook the snow from his sumptuous furs. Though small boned, like his royal brother, the Prince's flesh hung loosely and his face was puffed and white.

"Food," the High Priest was saying, "has been prepared for you. Though I fear it may be too plain for your taste."

Im-lo-Torim smiled. He had taken the precaution of bringing several boxes of sweetmeats and a cask of excellent wine.

"What satisfies your Holiness, satisfies me."

"It is Zeldin you must satisfy, not me," said the High Priest sharply.

He walked to the second litter and pronounced a formal welcome. The curtains did not open or even stir but Lord Izeldon heard the faint sound of bells and knew that the High Priestess had lifted her sistrum in greeting. He signed to the bearers to take up the closed litter and carry it into the heart of the temple.

"What keeps the Crown Prince?" murmured Izeldon.

Im-lo-Torim shrugged. "The Lady Gankali became faint and needs to rest. They will be here before moonrise."

"Come then," said the High Priest, "we have much to prepare."

Chapter 3

The Book of the Emperors: *Prophecy*

And the Holy House of Galkis shall be rent by hate and by the
jealousy of women. Then the Golden City shall lie beneath the
hand of doom and the stones of the temple shall weep blood.
Beware, beware, oh you of the Godborn. Let there be peace
between you, lest the star of Galkis be dimmed for ever!

IT was early evening when Forollkin at last strode into the
Prince's quarters. He was carrying a jar of ointment that
the High Priest had given him for Kerish. The table was
laid for a simple meal but the Prince was not in the outer
chamber. Forollkin flung open the bedroom door. He
might as well tell Kerish at once that he was leaving. He
marched into the bedchamber.

Kerish-lo-Taan lay curled on the bed, his face hidden by
tangled hair and pale hands. He was deeply asleep and
looked, as Forollkin had said, childish. Childish and vul-
nerable.

Disconcerted, Forollkin sat down rather suddenly on the
end of the bed. The movement disturbed Kerish. He
turned in his sleep on to his hurt shoulder and the pain
woke him. He opened his eyes to see Forollkin looking
down at him, the gash raw and dark on his cheek. Kerish
wondered just how angry his brother was as they stared at
each other in silence.

Then the Emperor's third son sat up very straight,
looked his half-brother in the eyes and said, "Lord Forollkin, for the injury I have done you I do not ask your forgive-
ness, for I know I do not deserve it. Therefore, I can only
offer up . . . my humblest apologies," he finished in a rush.

"I accept your apologies, Highness," answered Forollkin stiffly. "The High Priest sends you this ointment to

anoint your bruises." "Bruises got because of me," thought Forollkin, but his face did not alter.

"Thank you," said Kerish numbly, accepting the jar.

"When you've used it, supper is waiting." Forollkin walked to the door. "You had better hurry. It's only an hour till moonrise."

"Forollkin!" Kerish held out his hands. "Truly, I am sorry. Believe me . . ."

"Hurry," said his half-brother, "the priests will be here soon to help you robe."

He went out.

Kerish angrily tugged off his clothes. His right arm was almost too stiff to move and his legs were mottled with bruises. From an alabaster jar he scooped out the sticky ointment. With his left hand he rubbed it into his skin. It was cool and fresh and took away the ache of his bruises. Kerish put on a nightrobe of black fur and walked into the next room. Forollkin was staring into a half-drunk goblet of wine. With a great deal more difficulty than was apparent, Kerish sat down at the far end of the table.

There was silence.

At length, Kerish said, "Please pass the wine."

Forollkin did, and watched his half-brother pour out a full goblet before he spoke.

"I have been with Lord Jerenac."

"Have you?" said Kerish. He picked up a round, green fruit and began to peel it clumsily with his left hand.

"I shouldn't tell you this," began Forollkin again, "but the Five Kingdoms have signed an alliance."

Kerish understood the importance of the news but he showed no reaction.

"Have they?"

"I have just told you so," said Forollkin through gritted teeth. There was another silence during which Kerish struggled on with the fruit. When he dropped his knife for the third time, Forollkin could bear it no longer.

"Zeldin's mercy, let me do it for you, or we'll have you fainting from hunger during the ceremony."

"I can manage," said Kerish, but Forollkin took the plate away and cut up the fruit for him.

"Thank you," murmured Kerish. "Does your cheek hurt?"

"No," lied Forollkin, "does your arm?"

"Only a little." Kerish smiled hesitantly at his half-brother.

"Kerish," began Forollkin, "Lord Jerenac asked me to return with him to Jenoza. He wants me for his chief Captain and perhaps his heir."

"Then why do you look so sad?" asked Kerish cautiously. "You should be shrieking for joy."

"I have not given Jerenac his answer yet," replied Forollkin, "but tomorrow . . ."

"It is what you deserve, of course it is," began Kerish, "but perhaps . . ."

The door to their quarters swung open and a priest entered with two novices carrying a chest.

"Your Highness, my Lord, we are sent to help you to robe for the ceremony," announced the priest.

Kerish, his thoughts far away, thanked them and went into the bedchamber. The chest was opened and the Prince's ceremonial robes laid on the bed. As they were lifted out, leaving the chest dark and empty, Kerish shivered. His head began to ache, his skin was ice-cold to the touch. Everything he looked at seemed blurred and the voice of the priest was faint and remote.

Kerish knew the sensations and what they meant but they had never been so overpowering before. There was a darkness and a fear he could not name. Kerish remembered the face of Li-Kroch and tried to shut it out.

"Your Highness," repeated the priest gently. Kerish unfastened the clasp of his nightrobe and let it fall. When they had purified his body with scented water, he put on a plain light under-robe. Then the novices lifted the royal robe over his head and eased his bandaged arm, gently, into the sleeve. The robe fell in heavy folds to Kerish's ankles and the long sleeves swept the floor. The material was rich purple, stiff with embroidery in gold, silver and precious stones. It was too heavy to stand in for long but around the hem were woven the words: "As you bear the weight of this royal robe so bear the weight of your royal office."

31

On his feet they put silver sandals, whose soles were inscribed with the words: "Walk in the footsteps of Zeldin." One of the novices combed out the Prince's long, dark hair and the priest lifted up a circlet of cirge engraved: "Let your thoughts be one with Zeldin." In the centre of the circlet was a star-flower, symbol of the Godborn's divinity, carved in purple irivanee from the quarries of distant Proy, and with stamens of gold. The priest of Zeldin set it on the Third Prince's head and stepped back.

"Your Highness, it is done."

Kerish did not answer. He was too intent on trying to control the spreading darkness.

Forollkin came in. He had dressed hurriedly in a tunic of gleaming mail and a bright cloak. At his waist hung an ornamental dagger of chased gold and he carried a plumed helmet. He looked both splendid and uncomfortable but Kerish, white-faced and motionless in his glittering robe, seemed more like a tomb effigy than a living creature.

"Are you ready, Highness?" asked Forollkin.

"No." Kerish slowly shook his head. "No, I can't go."

"But you must," snapped Forollkin. "Are you ready?"

"I can't go out into that darkness."

"Kerish, there is no darkness."

"There is darkness everywhere, can't you see?"

Forollkin took his brother's wrist. "What is it? Is something going to happen?"

"I don't know," moaned Kerish. "There is only darkness."

Forollkin shook him gently. "I don't have your eyes. I can't see any darkness, but remember, it is nearly moonrise."

"Serene Highness," murmured the priest, "it is time; we must escort you to the main hall."

"Yes," sighed Kerish, "it is time."

The great hall of the temple, which that morning had been calm and empty, was now a different place. The room was shrouded with shadows and the air was thick with the scented smoke of incense. Priests carrying tapers passed to and fro in the dimness, their white robes whispering on alabaster. Inlaid in the centre of the floor were circles and arcs of silver, formed of ancient characters. Above them the roof of the hall swelled into a dome of clear crystal. In a half-moon before the circles, and facing the statue of Zeldin, were placed eight thrones for the royal guests.

By the time Kerish reached the hall he was calmer. A black bird still lodged in his mind but it was quiet enough to be forgotten, until it next dug in its claws. Forollkin kept very close to his half-brother, guiding him when he stumbled, for he still seemed to be walking in the darkness of his imagining. The young Captain wished that he could ask Izeldon's advice, but the High Priest, standing erect before the altar, a winged circlet gleaming on his brow, had no thoughts to spare for Kerish.

Beside him, a garish splash of colour against the soft darkness and shining whiteness, stood Jerenac. The Lord Commander was clothed in bronze mail with a cloak and overtunic of deep crimson. In his strong hands was a ceremonial sword of solid gold.

"Lord Jerenac, you cannot, I think, plead ignorance of the holy laws."

Jerenac smiled. "I am a plain soldier, Lord Priest, and know nothing of holiness."

"Then I will remind you, Lord Commander," said Izeldon, more gently. "If you bring a sword into the sanctuary of Zeldin, you must dedicate it to the god and never draw blood with it after."

"And what shall I do with a bloodless sword, when barbarians ravage the temples of Jenoza?"

"Zeldin will be your aid," answered the High Priest patiently, "but you know as well as I that you carry a ceremonial sword that would never taste blood in all its golden life. Its dedication will rob you of nothing but pride."

"Well then," snarled Jerenac, and threw the golden sword at Zeldin's feet. "And what will our Gentle God do with it? Destroy the hordes of the Five Kingdoms at a blow? Or challenge our Lady of Blood for the sovereignty of doomed Galkis?"

"If you refer to the new alliance . . ." began Izeldon.

"Teeth of Kir-Noac, who told you of that?"

"The eyes of Zeldin see far. I knew it before you did," answered the High Priest, "and I tell you this: if doom threatens Galkis, it is just. We have spurned our shield, the strength of Zeldin and the grace of Imarko. The chains of slaves darken the free cities, the people cry for justice and find none, the Godborn deny them even their faces, and temples and palaces bloat with treasures meant to be seen and shared. Little wonder we have sunk from our former greatness. Yet now, when our need is most grave, we must not become like the barbarians, we must not turn to the worship of their dark and bloody deities. If we gather our fears and our hopes and offer them up to Zeldin, he will save us yet. He will send us help!"

"Help?" Jerenac laughed again. "Do you speak of the old prophecy of the promised saviour? Your own scriptures say that he is imprisoned behind seven gates. Do I not tell the truth?"

"You do." Izeldon spoke as calmly as ever, but he was very pale.

"Then if Zeldin's saviour can be imprisoned by some other power," argued Jerenac, "that power must be greater than Zeldin, so why do we not worship it?"

"It would be better that the Golden City should fall!" Kerish broke in suddenly. He walked forward until he stood within the silver circles. "It would be better that the restless sea should destroy us all, than that the Godborn should betray their trust, that we should reject divinity and live on in darkness."

Straight and slender in his royal robes, Kerish faced the Lord Commander and it was Jerenac who first looked away.

"It is well enough for you, Prince, to choose godly defeat," muttered Jerenac, "but I am only a man and I would live, in darkness or in light."

Kerish's own darkness was lifting, he could almost feel light surging through his mind but it seemed to spill out as words.

"I do not speak of defeat. If we trust in Zeldin and Imarko we shall have victory, and surely a soldier knows that death with honour is better than life in slavery."

"Don't think I shun the path of honour," protested

Jerenac. "I only strive to save what I can by ways I understand."

"We honour you for that," answered Kerish-lo-Taan. "Nothing forbids us to defend ourselves, but the sword must be our last defence, not our first, and attack . . ."

"What is this?" interrupted a soft voice, "Do my Lords discuss heavy matters on such a joyful occasion as this?"

Kerish and Izeldon turned and Jerenac bowed to his half-sister.

Zyrindella smiled. As befitted an ascendant star, she blazed with jewels, yet the impression she created was one of soft darkness. Soft as those sponges of the Dirian sea that drown careless divers. Her robe of violet silk was weighted at hem and sleeve with gems set in ice-fire cirge. The high-collared bodice was stiff as a soldier's breastplate with rich embroidery. Her fine, black hair was divided into a hundred thin coils, each threaded with pearls. From a shining diadem hung a veil of finest purple gauze but it did not hide the glitter of the green-painted eyes. One thin, beringed hand rested on her husband's arm.

Li-Kroch had been made to drink zigul until he was docile enough to be groomed and dressed by his servants. Except for the eyes, he now seemed a presentable Prince and he stood quietly by Zyrindella as she spoke to the High Priest. With his mind clouded by zigul it was difficult to give even those unspoken orders that move an arm or turn a head. It was easier to accept the orders that came constantly from the harsh voices around him.

Yet no drug could wholly expel the fears which hid in the maze of his mind. Lying concealed, waiting for him to stumble past, were the birds, and their claws, their claws . . . Li-Kroch's wandering eyes were suddenly fixed on a terrifying object. In a niche in the alabaster wall squatted the figure of a bird, a zeloka, the messenger of Zeldin. No living zeloka now flew in Galkis but there, in gilded wood, glorious in its gold and purple plumage, sat the holy bird, and the claws of truth are very sharp. Li-Kroch stared and thought he saw the zeloka turn its razor-beaked head towards him. He tried to say, "Look, the bright bird!" but the words came out as a strangled moan.

35

Zyrindella tightened her grip on Li-Kroch's arm till her nails dug into his flesh.

"My husband is very tired," she said, "after the long journey."

Lord Izeldon turned to Kerish: "Will you take your cousin and his Princess to their places?"

Kerish nodded and the tense group by the altar broke up. He led Zyrindella to the crescent of alabaster thrones, speaking gently to Li-Kroch, who did not seem to hear.

Lord Jerenac strode after them, and Forollkin paused only to dedicate his own ceremonial dagger to the Gentle God.

Through the dim light he saw a flash of blue and silver as Lord Yxin entered.

"Why, your Highness," he said loudly to Kerish, "you hold your arm as stiffly as a tree in a gale. Does it pain you?"

Zyrindella turned quickly in her chair. "Dear cousin, are you hurt?"

"A small price his Highness paid for a lesson in the art of whipcraft," murmured Yxin.

Zyrindella ignored her half-brother and slid a hand up Kerish's arm. "Then take no more lessons, for a whip is more fitted to a herdsman than to a Prince! If you are in pain sit down by me. Cousin," she lifted her veil, "it is a long while since you visited us. We should be so glad to have you stay with us in Morolk; my husband is very fond of you . . ."

She prodded Li-Kroch, who made no response.

As Zyrindella talked, Yxin strode away and took his place at the far end of the crescent of thrones. Jerenac stood listening until Forollkin joined him.

"What's this I hear?" barked the Lord Commander. "Yxin gave your Prince a thrashing?"

"The Third Prince fought bravely, Sir, and for my sake."

"Well, boy, there's no need to splutter like water thrown on a fire."

"The High Priest signs to us," said Forollkin stiffly. "We had better take our places."

36

Jerenac grunted and sat down beside Yxin. Forollkin stood behind Kerish's chair, his heavy helmet crooked under his arm. Lord Izeldon was stationed by the altar and in an antechamber Lord Kor-li-Zynak, Prince Im-lo-Torim and the High Priestess of Imarko were waiting to enter.

"But wait we all must," thought Zyrindella bitterly, "until the Crown Prince deigns to join us!"

Still chattering lightly to Kerish, Li-Kroch's wife considered those present and noted those absent. After Zyrindella's mother had lost the Emperor's favour she had born a daughter and two sons to her husband, the Lord Governor of Tryfania, but only one of those children had been sent to represent the province at this ceremony. Still of the three, Yxin was the most likely to be won to her cause with promises of future power. He was sulking now but she could easily bring him round again and it might be important to cultivate the Third Prince.

Kerish-lo-Taan could prove dangerous if the rumours of the Emperor's affection for him were true. The first step would be to remove that cloddish Forollkin, then without his protection and influence ... Zyrindella's tongue curled round her painted lips.

The Governor of Hildimarn and the High Priestess had come, of course. Ka-Metranee was harmless enough, and for the moment Prince Im-lo-Torim's interests coincided with her own. Her idiot husband was trying to say something to Prince Kerish, something about birds. Zyrindella fingered her amethyst rings. The Emperor had not stirred from the Inner Palace, but she had expected that. Queen Rimoka had declared she could not leave her husband's presence — as if he did not hate the very sound of her footsteps.

Who else was missing? Only the Crown Prince's primary wife, meek Kelinda; no one of importance. There was satisfaction in Zyrindella's dark eyes. Soon all three Princes would be together in the temple. Three lives between the throne of Galkis and her son.

As even the High Priest began to look impatient, the doors to the great hall swung open. Everyone rose from their chairs. Zyrindella, her scowl hidden by the long, jewelled hair, curtsied low and the men of the Godborn knelt as the Crown Prince entered with his escort. Izeldon made no obeisance and said, "Welcome in the name of Zeldin, Master of the Moon, that waits for neither Prince nor beggar."

Prince Ka-Rim-Loka ignored this gentle rebuke and smiled lazily in greeting. Then he languidly saluted each of his relations in turn. Small and slight like his half-brothers, the Crown Prince seemed to find the weight of his golden robes insupportable and his magnificent diadem and long tasselled ear-rings were clearly giving him a headache.

No one, however, could be seated again before the Princess Gankali joined them and she was still kneeling before the image of Zeldin. Lord Izeldon helped her to rise for she was six months gone with her second child.

Gankali of Forgin, daughter of a merchant Prince, was decked in her dowry of jewels and precious silks. Around her neck, wrists and ankles hung heavy bands of red gold, set with huge, uncut gems. Coarse hair, the colour of dried blood, was coiled round her head and plaited with emeralds and pearls and her scent was stronger than the temple incense.

With little grace, the Crown Prince's second wife and the mother of his young daughter moved towards the crescent of thrones. Zyrindella, secure in the cold beauty of the Godborn, laughed silently at the gaudy, swollen figure. The men of the Godborn bowed but Li-Kroch's wife stood proudly beside the Crown Prince and did not curtsy.

In a high nervous voice, Gankali said, "I thought I was the Crown Prince's wife. The wife of the heir of Galkis, and his second Princess."

"No one denies it, my jewel," sighed Ka-Rim-Loka.

"One does," cried Gankali; "this Lady makes no obeisance. She means to slight me."

Zyrindella smiled. "I think, Highness, that you have not yet been able to learn all our ancient laws. This ceremony honours my son. On such an occasion the mother takes precedence over all royal ladies, so you should curtsy to me."

"To the daughter of a concubine," sneered Gankali.

"To the daughter of an Emperor, merchant's child," flashed Zyrindella.

"My ladies!" The High Priest approached them. "You forget that you stand in the House of God. Be seated and perhaps we shall be finished before the moon wanes."

But when Gankali was offered the throne next to Li-Kroch she raised her voice again.

Zyrindella's husband had not noticed the tensions around him. He had been too intent on watching the zeloka in its niche but now he smiled and stretched out his hands to Gankali.

"Rainbow Lady, purple, crimson, emerald, bright, bright, bright!"

The Princess backed away. "I can't sit next to that creature. You know I can't. You promised me he'd be drugged," whined Gankali. "You promised!"

Kerish was angry for his cousin's sake.

"Let Prince Li-Kroch sit between Princess Zyrindella and myself," he said, "and Your Highness between the Crown Prince and Lord Yxin."

Lord Izeldon smiled gratefully at Kerish and the Godborn changed thrones, as though they were playing some crazed game.

The High Priest returned to the altar and silver light poured through the watery crystal, turning white faces whiter and deepening the shadows.

Kerish felt a strange atmosphere gradually filling the hall that had nothing to do with the light or the incense or the jewelled figures beside him. It was more than an atmosphere, it was a presence, as if something vast and powerful was now contained within the fragile alabaster walls of the temple. The air seemed to thicken and press against Kerish's forehead. For a moment there was complete stillness and that moment might have lasted for eternity, while the glittering figures of the Godborn sat motionless in the pale moonlight. Then Lord Izeldon spoke: "Child of the Godborn, the full moon is risen. Come forth and face your destiny!"

Chapter 4

The Book of the Emperors: *Warnings*

*To lie is to insult both God and Zindar. For the world is made
from that which is and it is good. From that which is not, is
formed deceitful nothingness. Zeldin is truth. Untruth is darkness. To lie is to create darkness.*

Six white-robed priests preceded Kor-li-Zynak and six silver-clad priestesses walked behind, chanting the ancient moon hymn:

*The moon is a bright berry in the beak of the bird of dark-
ness.*
The moon is a jewel in the black hair of Imarko.
The moon is a lamp in the dark skies of eternity.

Zyrindella's son did not dare to look around him. He was nine years old and had travelled for many weeks to reach this high, cold place. All day he had been given nothing to eat and strangers had taken away his clothes and dressed him in a thin, white robe. His mother had told him again and again what he had to do, but it was difficult to remember.

On either side of the child walked Prince Im-lo-Torim and Princess Ka-Metranee. The Governor of Hildimarn was dressed more extravagantly than befitted a priest. His expression might have been taken for rapt devotion but the High Priest knew it for boredom. The High Priestess of Imarko was taller than her half-brother and very thin. Dull, black hair fell loosely to her ankles but her face was hidden by a purple veil. Few of the Godborn there had ever seen it, for she rarely left her sanctuary.

With faltering steps Lord Kor-li-Zynak reached the centre of the silver circles and remembered to stop. The six priestesses formed a wall of silver to his left, the line of priests stood to his right. Im-lo-Torim and his half-sister raised their hands and greeted the moon in the ancient Galkin tongue. Then they glided towards the thrones where the rest of the Godborn sat. Seeing his soft-spoken uncle move away, Kor-li-Zynak ran a few steps after him.

"Stand still, child," hissed the Governor of Hildimarn.

Kor-li-Zynak caught sight of his mother's face. He returned to the centre of the circles and turned his small back on the line of thrones. Now he faced the altar, the statue of Zeldin and the High Priest, who was smiling gently.

Zyrindella's little son stood shivering for nine minutes not daring to move, until Izeldon judged that the moon was exactly right. Then he was told to kneel before the statue of the Gentle God.

"Father of the House of Galkis," intoned the High Priest. "Most high Zeldin, here before you kneels a nameless child. If the blood of the Godborn runs truly in his veins, we beg you graciously to give us the ancient signs. If he bears none of the blood of the Godborn, then destroy him, even here in the House of Peace, for he has offered up a lie before your altar!"

There was deep silence but to Kerish it seemed that the presence had grown stronger. He could hardly bear the weight of it and yet the faces of the Godborn were calm, indifferent. It was not possible that they, too, felt what he did. He longed to cry out a warning but he knew his words would be stifled.

Lord Izeldon beckoned to a priest and priestess and they came forward each carrying a small golden sandal. Very carefully, the High Priest took them and held them up.

"Behold, all you who are gathered here, the very sandals of Mikeld-lo-Taan, first Emperor of Galkis, given to him in his ninth year by Zeldin the Bountiful. Come forward, child, put on the sandals, and as it was with Mikeld-lo-Taan, so shall it be with you, if the blood runs true."

He gave the sandals back to the priest and priestess and they put them on Kor-li-Zynak's feet.

"Now," commanded Izeldon, "walk!"

From the altar of Zeldin, Zyrindella's son walked unsteadily across what seemed a vast expanse of alabaster to where his uncle stood. When he reached him Im-lo-Torim said: "Let your steps be ever towards Zeldin."

When the child hesitated, he turned him round and gave him a slight push forward. Kor-li-Zynak stumbled back to stand within the silver circles. The High Priest and Im-lo-Torim walked towards each other along the path the child had taken. The Book of the Emperors related that with every step Mikeld-lo-Taan left behind him the clear imprint of his sandals, shining on earth or rock.

Kor-li-Zynak's footsteps glimmered faintly.

The High Priest and his great-nephew whispered together for a moment and then Im-lo-Torim said: "The sign is given."

After a pause, the High Priest repeated the words.

Zyrindella, who had been leaning forward, her own nails digging into her hands, sat back and smiled.

Lord Izeldon signed once more and two priests came forward, bearing between them something stiff and heavy; so heavy they could hardly lift it into the High Priest's waiting hands. Yet Lord Izeldon held up the small, glittering robe with no apparent difficulty.

"Behold, all you who are gathered here, the very robe of Mikeld-lo-Taan, given to him in his ninth year by Zeldin the Bountiful. Come forward, child, put on the robe, and as it was with Mikeld-lo-Taan, so shall it be with you, if the blood runs true."

To the High Priest the robe felt light as silk, but to those not of the Godborn it was heavy as sin. Izeldon eased the robe over Kor-li-Zynak's head. The child fell to his knees.

"The blood runs weak indeed," whispered Yxin to Jerenac, "as if on the mother's side only."

"Stand up," ordered the High Priest. Kor-li-Zynak staggered to his feet, his whole body aching with the weight of the robe. Lord Izeldon waited until the child had stood for seven long minutes, while Zyrindella coiled length after length of hair around her thin fingers.

Then slowly the High Priest said: "The sign is given."

Zyrindella laughed aloud, Gankali whispered to her

husband and Li-Kroch stared at the zeloka. The High Priest signed for quiet. Prince Im-lo-Torim, carrying a golden chalice, stepped into the silver circles. From the shadows opposite came Princess Ka-Metranee, a golden flask in her hand. Im-lo-Torim spoke: "Hail, Lady of the Moon. Lost in this desert named the world we seek the waters of heaven. As thy Foremother Imarko was the fountain of all compassion, so in her name do we beg you, quench our thirst."

The veiled Princess said nothing but poured from the flagon a rich purple liquid which filled the chalice.

Im-lo-Torim walked towards the High Priest, taking care not to spill a drop of the precious liquid, his thoughts flitting among the luscious orchards of Hildimarn.

"Child," ordered Izeldon. "Take the offered cup and drink without fear!"

The purple liquid contained the juice of a thousand starflowers, the irandaan, forbidden and fatal to any but the Godborn. His small hands shaking, Kor-li-Zynak took the chalice and raised it to his lips. Then he swallowed a mouthful of the irandaan. It was bitter and burned his throat.

"Again," ordered the High Priest, since for those with double Godborn blood it was safe to drink twice.

Kor-li-Zynak paused and then remembered his mother's smiling promise to have him whipped if he made any mistake. Zyrindella's son drank again, his throat scalded by the strength of the irandaan, nausea sweeping through his body.

Im-lo-Torim took back the chalice and offered it to the High Priest who drank deeply. Then, after drinking himself, he crossed to the crescent of thrones and offered it to each of the Godborn in turn. For form's sake, Gankali touched the rim of the chalice with her lips, but she could not drink. Then it came to Kerish and he sipped the irandaan with a shiver of excitement, for to him it tasted unbearably sweet and strong. Lastly, Im-lo-Torim offered the cup to Forollkin. He held the gold chalice to his lips but like Gankali he did not drink. He had tasted irandaan only once, at his own presentation, and he had found the effects

43

too frightening to repeat.

Im-lo-Torim returned to the altar and set down the empty chalice. Then he smiled at the High Priest.

"The tests are passed, my Lord, and the child is tired. Shall I pronounce the closing prayer?"

"No, the ceremony is not over." The High Priest spoke wearily. "It shall be performed according to the ancient law."

"But it is not now the custom to ask for any other sign," protested Im-lo-Torim.

"The ancient laws shall be obeyed," said the High Priest.

Forollkin did not understand the significance of Izeldin's words but he saw Zyrindella stiffen and Kerish turn to look at her.

"As it was in the time of Mikeld-lo-Taan, so shall it be now. Priest, inform the parents what they must do, unless you have forgotten the ritual."

Im-lo-Torim hastened across to the thrones and bowed to Zyrindella.

"Princess, the ritual of True Marriage and True Birth must now be performed. We must ask the god to give us a sign that Kor-li-Zynak is truly born of those who claim to be his parents."

White as chalk beneath her purple veil Zyrindella said: "But this was not done at Prince Kerish's presentation or . . ."

"Princess, it is the High Priest's command. Be calm, you have nothing to fear."

Zyrindella leashed her fears and said smoothly: "It will not be easy to teach my husband the ritual."

"It is very simple," soothed Im-lo-Torim, and he began to explain.

Zyrindella seemed calm but Kerish, his perceptions heightened by the irandaan, had sensed her wave of fear. The ominous presence was all around him. The black bird fluttered in his mind but he watched it happen as calmly as if the ceremony were a play performed by temple actors.

The great hall was flooded with thin, blue smoke as the priests and priestesses lit rods of the iranda incense that was burned on the marriage days of the Godborn. Izeldon

44

gently led Kor-li-Zynak to the altar and left him kneeling there. Then he signed for the ritual to being.

First Im-lo-Torim, his tasselled ear-rings swinging, walked into the centre of the circles. Izeldon touched his forehead saying, "By the will of the temple, he that stands here shall represent our Forefather Zeldin as he walked the earth of Galkis in the morning of the world."

Princess Ka-Metranee came forward. Izeldon touched her veiled forehead and pronounced, "By the will of the temple she that stands here shall represent our Foremother Imarko, as she walked the earth of Galkis in the morning of the world."

Izeldon stepped back. It seemed to Kerish that behind the small figures of Im-lo-Torim and his sister towered two vast, dark shadows, beautiful in shape and crowned with light. Izeldon saw them too and Ka-Metranee trembled beneath her veil.

"Behold, in the morning of the world," recited the High Priest, "the first men sailed across the purple sea and came to the empty lands. From the first ship stepped Imarko, fairest of maidens, and she walked upon the white shore."

Ka-Metranee moved across the silver circles.

"Then Zeldin, glorious in his solitude, came down the bridge of heaven into Zindar and he beheld Imarko."

As he spoke the ancient words, Im-lo-Torim and Ka-Metranee mimed them with slow, graceful gestures.

"The young god took her hand and swore that Imarko should be his only Lady and Queen. Never has that vow been broken and the firmament shall crack and the stars tumble into the seas before it ever shall be."

Ka-Metranee and Im-lo-Torim stood facing each other, their hands crossed, their palms touching in ritual embrace.

"To her and to her children Zeldin gave his wisdom and for her sake he cared for humankind. He who had been the Lord of Laughter became the Lord of Sorrows. Of this union was born Mikeld-lo-Taan, to whom his father gave the Empire of Galkis, to him and to his heirs for ever. Therefore, you of the Godborn, who take the sacred vows in Zeldin's temple, let your love and faith be no less than

45

that between Zeldin and Imarko."

Im-lo-Torim and his sister knelt, still touching palms. Kor-li-Zynak, alone by the altar, saw them through a haze of shadows. His skin burned as though he had a fever and there was something wrong with his eyes. The moonlight thickened and there were dark, threatening shapes drifting through the blue smoke. Kor-li-Zynak longed to run away but did not dare.

"Come, son and daughter of the Godborn," commanded the High Priest, "join with those who are the shadows of Zeldin and Imarko."

Zyrindella rose from her throne and took her husband firmly by the wrist. Li-Kroch was frightened and did not understand what they meant him to do, but he obeyed his wife's hissed commands. They came slowly forward and, parting, walked round the edge of the silver circles till they faced each other.

The zeloka now crouched in the shadows behind Li-Kroch. He longed to turn his head, to keep it in view, but he did not dare look away from Zyrindella's face.

"Behold, oh Zeldin," intoned the High Priest, "these thy children who were united before your altar twelve years ago. As of Zeldin and Imarko was born Mikeld-lo-Taan, so of Li-Kroch and Zyrindella is born Kor-li-Zynak."

The crowned shadows wavered. Kerish felt a faint tremor run through the temple, a tremor which, instead of dying away, gradually grew stronger until the floor hummed beneath his feet. No one else seemed to notice, no one but Ka-Metranee, who shook and swayed beneath her veils.

Li-Kroch and Zyrindella knelt and joined hands with Im-lo-Torim and Ka-Metranee. Together they recited the marriage vows they had sworn to obey. Zyrindella spoke clearly and surely, Li-Kroch with many stumblings and hesitations.

"As our blood is mingled so are our souls," finished Zyrindella.

The High Priest bade them rise and hand in hand they walked forward. For the first time Li-Kroch noticed his son. He smiled sweetly at him and spoke his name. Bright-eyed and flushed, the child did not seem to hear.

Once more Li-Kroch and Zyrindella knelt, this time before the image of Zeldin. The High Priest stood behind them and laid his long beautiful hands on their heads.

"Now," he said softly, "swear the oath."

Zyrindella's nails dug into her husband's hand but her face was calm.

"Speak after me," began Izeldon, "in one voice as you share one heart. I, the son or daughter of Zeldin, do swear that I have kept the holy law. I swear that the bird of Truth still lodges in my house. I swear that I am true in marriage and in faith and that Kor-li-Zynak is the true born son of our marriage."

Li-Kroch began to mouth the words without understanding but Princess Zyrindella spoke them clearly and proudly.

"I, the daughter of Zeldin, do swear that I have kept the holy law."

The hall of the temple throbbed as if it was a drumskin, stretched too tight, on which some giant hand was beating. The priests and priestesses stopped their chanting and Im-lo-Torim ran forward.

"Go on," commanded the High Priest.

"I swear," whispered Zyrindella, "that the bird of Truth still lodges in my house. I swear that I am true in marriage and in faith."

The temple shook. Dark cracks appeared in the alabaster and the crystal dome shivered. Zyrindella screamed in defiance: "And I swear that Kor-li-Zynak is the true born son of our marriage."

As suddenly as the damping of a taper, moonlight became darkness. The very rocks beneath the temple moved. The alabaster pillars swayed, the walls groaned. The air seemed to press against Zyrindella until she thought her skull would crack. It was impossible to breathe, for there was no emptiness left in the great hall.

In the blackness Gankali screamed again and again and the Crown Prince could not quiet her. Yxin and Jerenac sprang to their feet and Im-lo-Torim raised his voice in

47

wailing prayer.

Kerish alone sat calm and still and Forollkin clung to his chair. Nine times the temple shuddered. Then above the tumult rang out the High Priest's voice, speaking in the ancient tongue.

There was silence and stillness and very slowly the moonlight flooded back into the hall. It revealed no scene of devastation. The cracks in the smooth floor had closed. The crystal dome was intact and the statue of Zeldin smiled as serenely as ever.

Among the alabaster thrones huddled Gankali, crying hysterically. Kerish, Forollkin, Yxin and Jerenac had stayed where they were, unharmed, but in the darkness and confusion the Crown Prince had fled from the hall.

Im-lo-Torim and the priests and priestesses had prostrated themselves before the altar. Ka-Metranee alone stood upright within the silver circles.

"Hear, all you of the Godborn," cried Izeldon, "a lie has been offered before the very altar of Zeldin!"

He looked down at Zyrindella, and she cowered before him.

"You are false to your vows, to your husband and to yourself. Be gone, daughter of lies. Zeldin has spoken and I banish you both from the temple and the court. Go!"

Zyrindella gathered up her jewelled robe and fled from the hall.

Izeldon strode after to give orders for an escort to take her north to Morolk.

At the feet of Zeldin's statue lay the small, crumpled figure of Kor-li-Zynak. While the temple shook his eyes had seen terrible shapes among the shadows. With a voiceless scream he had fallen unconscious. The strength of the irandaan had overwhelmed him.

Li-Kroch understood nothing of what had happened, not even that Kor-li-Zynak was not his son. He saw the child fall and ran to him. Li-Kroch cradled the little boy in his arms, rocking him and soothing him.

"Little one, wake up, the darkness is all gone."

The child lay still and his skin burned to the touch. Li-

Kroch tried again to rouse him and then cried out: "The birds have torn my little one with their claws. They have eaten his soul. The bright birds..."

He gently laid the child down and picked up the empty chalice from the altar steps.

"The birds," he hissed, "the birds who laugh at tears. I will kill them, every one."

Too late, Kerish sprang from the chair and ran forward. Before the Prince could reach him, Li-Kroch had thrown the heavy chalice at the zeloka. The sacred bird was knocked from its niche and as it hit the floor the frail wood shattered into gilded splinters. Li-Kroch laughed in triumph but Ka-Metranee, High Priestess of Imarko, screamed and threw back her purple veil.

"Sacrilege!" she cried.

In her gaunt face blazed huge, inhuman eyes.

"Sacrilege! Sacrilege!"

The cry echoed round the temple. The Godborn stood silent, aghast, staring at the fragments of the holy bird. Only Gankali still crouched by the thrones.

Li-Kroch's wild laughter died on his lips as he saw the Godborn turn one by one to look at him. He whimpered with fright at the expression in Ka-Metranee's eyes.

"The birds, the bright birds..." and huddled by the altar, Li-Kroch lifted the child in his arms again.

The High Priestess knelt among the splinters and picked up the golden chalice. She clasped it to her breast and gave a low cry of agony.

"Sacrilege!" she whispered. "The bird of Wisdom shall fly no more in Galkis, the bird of Truth is dead, murdered in Zeldin's temple."

She walked to the centre of the circles and stood beneath the dome, pale as a drowned corpse in the moonlight.

"From this chalice," said Ka-Metranee, "you have drunk the irandaan, the gift of Zeldin. I tell you, when you drink from it again, it shall be of your own blood. For the blood of the Godborn shall run like rivers. Murder!" Her voice rose to a scream. "Murder and war in the Holy City. The Godborn shall tear out their own hearts and the throne of Galkis shall be stained with their blood. Death and darkness come to the Golden City. The Empire shall fall and the nine cities crumble. Weep, oh weep, for the glory of Galkis is dimmed for ever!"

The priestess, her long, black hair trailing the ground, turned on those who stood nearest to her.

"Death, I see only death."

She pointed to Jerenac and Yxin. "To you a sword, and to you a dagger, forged by your own hands."

She faced Im-lo-Torim and Gankali. "To the cowardly, a coward's death, and for you who killed the bird of Truth," Li-Kroch cowered before her, "you shall be starved of more than wisdom."

Lastly, she turned on Forollkin and Kerish. To the young soldier she said: "Yours is a long road, the hard road of sorrow, and you..." Looking at Kerish, for the first time she faltered. "Your death is strange and distant and I cannot see it clearly, but for the rest of you there shall be murder. Cursed are the rulers and cursed are the ruled. Cursed is Golden Galkis and cursed are the Godborn!"

"No," cried Lord Izeldon. "No!" He strode the length of the hall until he stood before the priestess of Imarko. "All may come to pass as you prophesy, but in Zeldin the Compassionate there is hope. What is promised will be given, if we ask, if we seek."

The fire of prophecy died from Ka-Metranee's eyes. Her face became gentle, her voice meek.

"You speak of the Promised One?"

"I do."

The High Priestess began to weep. "But who will seek him out? Who will free him from his prison?"

"Sister, the moon has waned, the ceremony is over. Go now and pray to our Lady Imarko for mercy."

Ka-Metranee curtsied low and cast her veils back over her face. She called gently to her cowed priestesses and left the hall.

Kerish was kneeling by Li-Kroch and the child, trying to comfort them. Izeldon came and took the child's hand and felt his brow.

"Will he live, my Lord?" whispered Kerish.

"Yes," sighed Izeldon, "but I fear that after tonight he

50

may seem like Li-Kroch's son indeed."

The High Priest would have taken the child in his arms but Li-Kroch would not let him go. So Izeldon called his trembling priests and ordered them to take Li-Kroch and the child to the temple Healers.

Im-lo-Torim had controlled his face again and was longing for a draught of Tryfanian wine to cool his seared nerves. He hurried forward when the High Priest beckoned him.

"Take the Princess Gankali to her chambers and see her tended. If you find the Crown Prince there tell him to visit me in the morning."

Smiling at that, Im-lo-Torim led the still sobbing Gankali from the hall.

"Lord Priest," Jerenac laughed uneasily, "perhaps your god is not so gentle as I thought."

"Lord Commander, the anger of Zeldin is turned against us, not our enemies. Your prayers are needed."

Jerenac bowed and strode out. Yxin turned to follow him but asked, "Your Holiness, now the Princess is banished from court, will she lose her province too?"

"Child," said Izeldon gravely, "I judge her only for sacrilege. The Emperor may punish her other crimes if he chooses, that is his burden."

When Yxin had gone, the High Priest spoke to Kerish:

"My dear, thank you for your help this night. In the morning, come to me early and we will talk. Now both of you, sleep peacefully. I know you are tired."

He watched Kerish and Forollkin go, and then knelt wearily before Zeldin's statue.

In their quarters Kerish and Forollkin disrobed in silence. When their attendants had gone Kerish sank into the drowsy calm that comes after extremes of emotion but Forollkin said suddenly, "Kerish, I'm sorry I can't stay. I must get away."

He was white and trembling with delayed shock. The Prince poured out a cup of strong, red wine and gave it to his half-brother.

"It's all right now. Zeldin would never harm you.

You're a truth speaker if ever there was one."

"I can't stay," insisted Forollkin. "The palace chokes me, the city chokes me, and the temple..."

Kerish laughed unkindly. "I'll protect you from the wrath of Zeldin, my brave soldier."

"You don't understand," cried Forollkin. "How can you protect yourself from something you can't even see. How do you fight?"

"I don't know," said Kerish-lo-Taan.

Chapter 5

The Book of the Emperors: *Wisdom*
*A man enters life by the Gate of Birth and leaves it by the Gate
of Death. Between stand many gateways, some open, some
shut, some locked fast. The end of wisdom is to open the closed
gates to find the keys of those that are locked, and to know what
lies beyond them.*

Kᴇʀɪsʜ had slept for barely six hours when the High
Priest's messenger woke him. To his alarm, Forollkin
was already gone from his hard couch and his travelling
cloak was missing. Uneasily the Prince dressed. The High
Priest's ointment soothed his bruises but his arm was stiff
and sore.

The messenger led him to an unfamiliar part of the
temple: the place to which the grievously sick or wounded
were carried in litters, up the mountain road from Galkis.
Kerish found the High Priest sitting by Kor-li-Zynak's
bed. The child was still unconscious but there was natural
colour in his cheeks and his skin no longer burned. Izeldon
had sat with him all through the night, trying to call him
back from the darkness into which he had fled.

As the Prince entered the chamber Izeldon looked up and
smiled but Kerish thought for the first time that the High
Priest showed his eighty years. His serene face was giving
way at last to the attacks of time.

"Good morning, Kerish. I hope I have not summoned
you too early?"

Kerish stifled a yawn. "No, my Lord. How is the
child?"

"At rest now. The damage to his mind is not so great as I
feared but the irandaan will leave shadows."

"Holiness," Kerish looked down at the small form of

Kor-li-Zynak, "you knew, I think, that he was not Li-Kroch's son and yet you let him drink a double dose of irandaan. You must have guessed what would happen to him. Why should he suffer for his mother's sins?"

"I guessed, Kerish, but I was not certain. No one could be, until it was tried before Zeldin's altar. If Zyrindella were no more than an adulteress I should be little inclined to blame her. Such a marriage, however much her own choice, must be bleak and bitter, but I have read murder in her eyes. I had to prove her false to protect us all. Yet you are right, to risk an innocent child was wrong and I must carry my sin till Zeldin has mercy."

"I understand," said Kerish, "truly I do. You look so tired, can't you rest now?"

"That is a kind thought, Kerish, and you have an aching arm. Let us have breakfast together and see which of our ills may be mended."

Izeldon gave the Healers orders about the tending of Kor-li-Zynak and then took Kerish to his quarters. There the High Priest examined Kerish's arm, which was healing cleanly, and bathed it again. While he did so the Prince asked after Li-Kroch.

"He is bewilder~ᵈ still," answered Izeldon. "Since he loves the child it is better that they remain together and away from Zyrindella. I will ask the Emperor's permission for them to live in the Royal Lodge. There now, fasten your tunic and we will drink together."

Izeldon fetched a flagon and poured a thin, golden liquid into two alabaster goblets. They sat down together on the windowsill.

"Sip slowly, Kerish, this wine is called the Blood of the Sun and it will give you strength. It was a gift from Elmandis, the King of Ellerinonn. Have you heard stories of the Seven Sorcerers?"

Kerish nodded.

"He is one of them," continued Izeldon, "perhaps the greatest, and beautiful Ellerinonn is ringed by his power and protected from all harm. I suppose your tutors have taught you almost nothing of foreign lands?"

"They have taught me about our Empire; surely that is

enough."

"No, it is not! Too often we think of Galkis as the heart of Zindar, but there is a world beyond our borders, different countries, peoples, gods."

"False ones?"

"That you must judge for yourself," said Izeldon, with a curious half smile, "though do not tell your tutors I said so. Always remember, Kerish, that you are only partly Galkian; your mother came from Erandachu."

"Dragged from it as a slave."

"That was our shame not hers," said Izeldon sternly. "In her own country she was the daughter of a great chieftain and you must not be denied half of your heritage. You should learn about her people, the Erandachi, the Children of the Wind, and about many others.

"Beyond Galkis lie Lan-Pin-Fria, the Land of Four Rivers; Everlorn, the secret forest; fair Seld, where Kelinda's sister is Queen; the jewelled deserts of Kolgor; Gannoth, the Isle of Enchantments, where your grandmother was born . . ."

"And the Five Kingdoms," murmured Kerish.

"Yes, there are dark places, too, beyond Galkis," agreed Izeldon. "The slave quarries of Proy; the pleasure gardens of Losh; the dead kingdom of Roac; the black temple of Azanac . . . but in truth no land is wholly good or bad."

"I wish I *could* see them," said Kerish, "but I've never even been to Viroc or Morolk. What chance do I have of seeing the Great Ocean?"

"A chance you may take by speaking one word."

Kerish set down his cup and stared at the High Priest.

"But the Godborn are forbidden to leave Galkis!"

"Without the Emperor's permission, yes, but I think you would have it."

"He wants me to go away?" asked Kerish, bewildered.

"We both do," said Izeldon. "If I had had my way, you would have been sent to the safety of Gannoth or Seld years ago, but your father loved you too much. Never think that because you see him so rarely, the Emperor does not watch over you. Still, that is past; it is the future we have to struggle with."

The High Priest got up from the window seat and paced his narrow chamber.

"We talked yesterday of the Promised Saviour and our prophets tell us that he may only be freed by one of the Godborn." Izeldon paused for a moment and then spoke with quiet intensity. "Kerish-lo-Taan, you must seek him, you must open the Seven Gates and destroy his prison!"

"Me? But how?" stammered Kerish. "Why me?"

"There are two reasons," said Izeldon. "First, tell me what you felt last night."

Kerish answered slowly and carefully.

"Before the ceremony, darkness and fear. I knew that something terrible was going to happen and that there was nothing I could do to prevent it."

Izeldon nodded and spoke very gently. "It is not quite as bad as it seems. You are not, like Ka-Metranee, cursed with the gift of prophecy."

"Then why . . .?"

The High Priest would not let him ask. "Go on, Kerish."

The orchids in the silver bowl were dying. Kerish fingered their brittle petals as he spoke.

"Then the darkness was driven out by something else, a power all around me, filling the whole temple. I suppose you will call it Zeldin, but what right does he have to come inside my head?"

An orchid shivered into dust as his fingers clenched it.

"If he had stayed much longer, I would have lost myself in him."

"As I am lost," murmured Izeldon.

Kerish would not look at him. "But to be forced to submit! If Zeldin can use such power against us, how can we pretend to be free?"

Izeldon sighed. "You will find that pride is a strong defence, even against Zeldin. We are free to refuse or accept, and our god offers payment for everything he takes from us."

"But if we need him," persisted Kerish, "we can never be free."

The High Priest did not answer and Kerish asked, almost timidly, "My Lord, now you know how I feel, do you still want me to seek the Promised Saviour?"

"Yes, it is still your quest, but Kerish-lo-Taan, I tell you this," said Izeldon, "you are arrogant and quick-tempered. Unless you humble your pride and curb your temper others besides you will suffer for it and your quest will fail; the hope of Galkis will be extinguished because of you."

"My Lord, you are unfair!" gasped Kerish. "You said yourself that my brothers, my sister, even my father, are dragging Galkis towards darkness. How can I be solely to blame?"

Izeldon looked down into the Prince's defiant face. "Because you are young. You still have the power to heal yourself. For the others, I fear it is already too late."

Kerish's colour rose. "Then you are choosing me because there is no one else?"

Izeldon did not deny it. "Yes. The need is desperate now. Im-lo-Torim will soon be High Priest and I know that, in his lack of faith, he will betray our ancient trust."

"But that won't be for many years!" protested Kerish.

Izeldon shook his head. "In less than two years, I shall be dead. Don't look so stricken, child. I am not Zeldin, I cannot live for ever."

"But won't you fight against death?" demanded Kerish.

"No." Izeldon smiled. "I know it must seem strange to you, who are young and born to argue with everything. That is an uncomfortable quality, but a good one for your quest. In spite of your faults, I trust you to succeed. You will, however, need help. Forollkin now..."

Kerish interrupted. "My Lord, have you seen him? He was gone when I woke up and I'm afraid he's with Jerenac."

"I saw him pacing the bronze courtyard at dawn," answered Izeldon, "with nothing but his thoughts for company."

"Lord Jerenac wants Forollkin to return to Jenoza with him," explained Kerish. "But if you give orders..."

"There will be no orders," said Izeldon gravely. "Forollkin will make his own choice, as you must."

"I have already decided," declared Kerish. "I will go!"

"No!"

Kerish could not read the strange expression on the High Priest's face.

"No!" repeated Izeldon. "You cannot choose yet. You must listen to the Emperor; he will tell you what your life will be like if you remain in Galkis."

"Would this quest take us far beyond Galkis?" asked Kerish. "Who imprisons the Saviour and why?"

"I do not know," said Izeldon flatly.

Kerish stared at him in astonishment. "Then how can we even begin?"

Somewhere in the temple bells were ringing. Light flooded through the tall windows cleansing the stains of tiredness from the High Priest's face.

"There is some knowledge handed down across the centuries from High Priest to High Priest. Kerish, you must understand how dangerous this quest could be. If you leave Galkis you may never return. You accused me of sacrificing Kor-li-Zynak to trap Zyrindella. Are you not afraid that I will let you suffer too for the sake of Galkis?"

"I think you might let me suffer," said Kerish, "but not without fair warning. My Lord, I trust you also."

"I am too old for such gifts." Izeldon's tone was almost bitter. "But if you mean what you say, then do not repeat our conversation to anyone, not even to Forollkin, and you must leave for Galkis at once. I have sent a message to Forollkin; your litter is waiting for you in the outer courtyard. Tomorrow you will receive a summons from the Emperor and we shall talk again."

He leaned forward to kiss Kerish's forehead: "Go now with Zeldin's love."

Forollkin fixed Kerish's standard to his saddle bow and waited, keeping a tight grip on the reins of his restless horse. He had argued for a long while with the High Priest's messenger. He had told him several times that he had promised to talk to Lord Jerenac later that morning. Courteously, but firmly, the priest had ordered him to collect his belongings and wait in the outer courtyard for his Prince. They were to leave for Galkis at once.

Forollkin found the escort waiting and his roan mare stamping and snorting in greeting. The men noted a new scar on their captain's cheek and whispered among themselves. They had heard nothing of the events of the ceremony; for them no darkness had fallen and the temple had not been shaken but the sudden departure of Zyrindella had not gone unremarked.

Cloaked and veiled in black, Kerish entered the courtyard, attended by several priests. He saw Forollkin's expression and, ignoring the waiting litter, crossed to his half-brother.

Kerish smiled wearily: "Forollkin, you look as chafed by time as I feel. I had hoped we could rest today, but the High Priest will have us go back to Galkis and nothing I could say would make him change his orders."

Forollkin saw the shadows under his brother's brilliant eyes. "You look as frail as the first ice of winter," he said. "Does your arm pain you?"

"A little," murmured Kerish. "I know you meant to leave me today Forollkin, but I'm afraid you must be patient until we're home. Then I shan't hold you back from your fortune. I will wish you joy and . . ."

Kerish's voice trembled.

"I've given no answer to Lord Jerenac yet," said Forollkin gruffly.

"You haven't spoken to him?"

"I was to have met him in his quarters after the tenth bell but now . . ."

"Oh Forollkin, I'm so sorry!" exclaimed Kerish. "Shall I ask one of the priests to take a message to the Lord Commander?"

"I've sent one already, though why you should care if . . ."

Kerish blazed at him: "I care very much for my brother's happiness! Even if he doesn't, doesn't . . ."

Kerish turned suddenly and half ran to his litter, leaving Forollkin bewildered and faintly guilty.

The Prince stepped into his litter and drew the curtains close. After a moment Forollkin realized that his men were all staring at him, and gave the order to move off. As the bearers lifted the litter, Forollkin mounted and spurred his horse out of the courtyard without looking back at the temple, as white softened into gold in the morning sunlight.

Kerish settled down among the cushions, smiling to himself.

The Prince's escort clattered down and down the marble road, the sound of hooves and feet ringing through the stillness of the Holy Mountain. The road was so steep that it seemed possible, with one false step, to walk right off the mountain. Gradually the great plain of Galkis came into view. In the space of an hour the purple distance of the farmlands appeared, then the glittering coils of the river Gal and lastly the Golden City itself. It was a city of ninety thousand people but from above it seemed as lifeless as a golden jewel dropped by a careless giant.

The road dipped below a ridge and spiralled down into the valley of the Royal Lodge. The plain of Galkis vanished from sight. The escort passed quickly through the sheltered valley, not stopping for a rest or refreshment at the Lodge. The road wound down through a country of stark rock. The way became narrow and tortuous, leading along ravines and gorges and across bridges wet with the spray of streams swelled to torrents by the spring rains. A zeloka could have flown from the Royal Lodge to the foothills above Galkis in less than two hours, but the journey took the Prince's escort the greater part of the day.

Kerish slept through most of it and woke just before sunset to the sound of Forollkin rapping out orders.

"Any man who speaks or makes a sound will lose his place in the Prince's guard."

Kerish drew back the curtains and looked out. Forollkin was binding his horse's muzzle so that it could not neigh or whicker. The pack-horses had been treated in the same way and the soldiers were carrying their swords and daggers in case they clinked against their mail as they walked.

"Now forward," ordered Forollkin, "and nobody speak until I give the signal!"

The escort had halted before a sheer cliff, through which the road ran in a narrow ravine. As they moved forward

Kerish sat up, fully awake. Slowly, they passed along a road so dark they could hardly see two paces ahead. Within minutes they had reached a high arch carved from the rock, and light again. Light in the Valley of Silence, for to reach Galkis they had to pass above the ancient burial ground of the Godborn.

Beyond the archway lay a deep, sheltered valley. Their road wound along a narrow ledge half-way up the cliffs that divided the valley from the world of the living. The Prince's escort passed under the archway into utter and oppressive silence. They moved cautiously but swiftly along a path thick with grass that muffled the horses' hooves.

Kerish leaned from the swaying litter to look down. The lush valley below was studded with iranda, the flowers that sprang up wherever Zeldin had walked. Millions of purple flowers, each with five petals in the shape of a star and a glorious golden heart. The rich scent of them thickened the air. The silence was solid, tangible, terrifying. Kerish felt that the slightest sound would wake some great force that lay dormant all about them.

While Kerish looked down, Forollkin and the escort hurried on, keeping their eyes on the ground. When one of the Godborn died it was here, to this silence, that they were brought. Dressed in their bridal clothes, they were laid in shallow, unmarked graves among the iranda flowers.

One day, all his warring family, Gankali and Zyrindella, Queen Rimoka and the Emperor would lie side by side in those nameless graves, sharing the same peace. At that strange thought, heedlessly, Kerish laughed aloud. His laughter was swallowed by the inexorable silence but Forollkin and the escort froze in horror. Seeing their faces, Kerish wished he could take back the sound and suddenly the impossibility of winning anything back from the past struck him like a blow. He might have changed his life by this single action and there was nothing he could do but abide by the consequences.

"If you leave Galkis you may never return," Izeldon had said. Had he doomed himself by his swift, thoughtless answer, "I will go"? For a long minute the Prince and his escort waited for the earth to gape or the mountains to fall, but there was only stillness and the liquid gold of sunset. Breathing deeply, Kerish signalled to Forollkin to go on.

Forollkin was too angry to speak to his brother again until the outskirts of Galkis were in view. Kerish had frightened him badly. It was dark now, but the road was lit by flaring torches in the hands of bronze statues. The city of Galkis was ringed with three great walls and the outer wall of white Tryfanian marble was pierced by four gates. They stood open day and night, for the city had never known attack or siege. As Kerish and his escort passed through the temple gate, trumpets sounded and his name was called out from herald to herald.

The Outer City was very different from the Galkis founded by Mikeld-lo-Taan three thousand years before. Except for the straight road which led towards the Palace, its streets were narrow, winding and dark. Small, over-crowded houses clustered together, built of dank, grey stone with black slits for windows. In the cool of evening, most households gathered together on the flat roofs of their homes to eat the after-sunset meal or to sing the sweet melancholy airs of a lost splendour, known and beloved by all Galkians.

Those few people still on the streets knelt down and bowed their heads until the Prince's litter had passed. Kerish looked at the fellow citizens to whom he had never been allowed to speak, and who would never see his face unveiled. Their half-seen faces were sullen and pale and he wondered how much love and loyalty they had left for the Godborn. Here, in these people, could be a reason for staying in Galkis.

"Can I really help them more by leaving?" wondered Kerish.

"Highness," hissed Forollkin, "keep the curtain drawn while we're in the Outer City."

Kerish sighed and lay back among the cushions. No one yet starved in Galkis, but poverty darkened the Golden City. Kerish shut out the sight.

The great stones of the middle wall were covered by sheets of silver, marvellously engraved with images of former Emperors and texts from the scriptures. The trumpets sounded and the gate itself, inlaid with huge slabs of lapis, was unbarred and opened. Beyond lay the gracious Middle City and the homes of the nobles and the artists and craftsmen so highly honoured in Galkis. The houses which faced the Palace road were built of polished stone ornamented with fine carvings, but many were empty and decaying. Silver tiles fell from the rooftops, gardens grew wild, statues crumbled and paved courtyards were rank with weeds.

To pass through the Middle City took nearly an hour but at last they reached the third wall and Kerish sat up and opened the purple curtains. No matter how many times he had seen the inner wall, it was not enough to absorb its beauty. The high rampart was covered with pure, dazzling gold, that blazed like fire in the torchlight and the words of Zeldin circled the city in characters twice the height of a man, picked out in precious gems. Down the centuries men had travelled from all over Zindar, just to gaze at that splendour.

For the third time trumpets sounded for Kerish and the gate of ivory and irivanee, worth an Emperor's ransom, swung open. Inside lay the Outer and Inner Palaces of the Emperor of Galkis and his court of three thousand people. All but the litter bearers were dismissed and the horses were led away. Forollkin walked beside the Prince's litter as it was carried through a succession of splendid courtyards towards the final gate. There they were challenged by the Imperial Guard, resplendent in purple and gold. Forollkin was a Captain in that same guard, and it was he who replied.

"Open for his Serene Highness, Prince Kerish-lo-Taan, Third Son of the Emperor of Galkis, may his reign be eternal!"

The guard bowed to the ground, the gate opened and Kerish and Forollkin were absorbed into the rich stillness of the Inner Palace, the heart of Golden Galkis.

Forollkin did not go immediately to his own quarters on the north side of the Prince's courtyard, but visited a silver-roofed pavilion in the area of the Palace reserved for royal concubines.

By the delicate light of tapers, in a room hung with rich tapestries and crowded with furniture and ornaments, a woman sat embroidering. She wore no veil. Her dark brown hair, just tinged with grey, was braided severely and her heavy dress was plain, without jewels. She looked up as the door opened and a young slave curtsied to her.

"Lord Forollkin is returned, my Lady."

"Then bid him come in," said Follea calmly.

She had heard the trumpets sounding for Prince Kerish-lo-Taan and knew that where he was her son would be also.

Forollkin strode into the small, cluttered room and kissed his mother on the forehead. With a sharp cry she thrust him back.

"Zeldin's mercy, what have you done to your cheek?"

"Just an accident, Mother," said Forollkin, unthinkingly masking the wound with his hand.

Follea turned to her slave: "Fetch us some food and the white wine of Indiss."

"Your words are my actions," answered the girl and left them alone together.

"And now, Forollkin, what manner of accident?"

Her son slung down his travelling cloak and perched on an ebony stool to pull of his boots.

"Lord Yxin was at the temple, playing bloody games with a hide whip."

"He struck you!"

Leaning over his boots Forollkin muttered, "No, not him."

Follea heard. "I knew it. Proud Prince Kerish, the vicious . . ."

"Mother, his temper slipped its leash, that's all. He was sorely provoked by Yxin and he gave me his apologies very humbly."

Follea laughed harshly. "The seas will quench the stars before the Godborn are humble and Kerish-lo-Taan is the worst of them all, slave-girl's son though he is."

"A slave girl who supplanted you in the Emperor's affections," thought Forollkin. He knew well enough why his mother hated Kerish-lo-Taan, but he valued his peace too much to argue against it. "There is no malice in the Prince," he said mildly.

"I think otherwise," snapped Follea, "but come, what other news do you have?"

"I spoke with Lord Jerenac," answered Forollkin cautiously.

Follea looked at him sharply. "He thinks well of you, as I have heard."

"Mother, he wishes me to return with him to Jenoza," said Forollkin abruptly. "He hinted that I would succeed him as Lord Commander."

"Oh, my son!" Follea embraced him hungrily. "That is the best news you could have brought me. Lord Commander of Galkis, it sounds well. I do not doubt that your sword will carve out glory for you and for your mother!"

"Mother, Mother," Forollkin held her away from him, "I haven't given Lord Jerenac my answer yet. I am not sure . . ."

"Not sure, when fortune stares you in the face! Are you mad?"

"Mother, there is Kerish . . . Jenoza is a long way from the Palace and such a parting would hurt him deeply. He is young and alone and he still needs my help."

"He may need you," retorted Follea, "but what has he done to deserve you? He uses you, and when he can no longer use you he will toss you aside like a withered fruit whose juices he has sucked dry. His father, all the Godborn, are the same. You must think of your own life, and if not of yours, then of mine."

Forollkin knew what she would say next. "I am your mother who carried you in her body, but you never think of me. You refuse an offer that would give *me* honour and cling to your precious Prince, while *I* must serve a foreign Queen. You will care nothing if I die destitute among strangers."

Forollkin glanced at the tapestries, the elegant furniture, the silken robe she was embroidering for herself.

"Mother, I have not yet chosen, and I must have silence

to make my decision."

"But how can I trust you to know what is best?" cried Follea. "You do not have the cunning of the Godborn."

The door opened and two slaves entered carrying a flagon of wine, a steaming dish of spiced meat and a bowl of fruit. They set them down on a table, bowed and withdrew. Forollkin suddenly realized how hungry he was. Follea, her face calm again, picked up her embroidery.

"When you have eaten," she said, "you must tell me your other news. Did the ceremony go well?"

Kerish-lo-Taan was met in his apartments by four of the ever-changing servants who waited on him. He stood passively while they stripped off his travelling clothes and then washed in the scented water they brought him and put on a loose, silk robe and jewelled sandals.

On a square table a splendid supper had been laid out on bowls and platters of delicate gold. Kerish, who hated being watched as he ate, sat down in an uncomfortable ivory chair and picked at his meal, impaling slivers of meat on a silver fork. His servants stood silently at the four corners of the table. Not for the first time he found himself almost afraid of them. He had no idea how to break into their world and make them see him as a person instead of a daily task.

He glanced round the familiar apartments; at the tall windows opening on to the garden, the hanging lamps of translucent alabaster, the marble floor inlaid with golden stars and spread with soft black furs . . . the events of the temple seemed very remote.

The lonely evening stretched before him, like so many others. A Prince of the Godborn was too exalted to have friends; there was only his family to cling to. Kerish took refuge in beautiful things, the precious objects that made the room exclusively his own: the vase of gold-veined lapis that held the Emperor's weekly gift of a rare orchid; the casket of creamy ivory, decorated with zelokas strutting among starflowers, that housed his copy of the Book of Emperors; his zel set; and most of all, his zildar, a seven stringed instrument, delicately carved, and painted in purple and gold.

When supper was cleared away he practised the zildar for a while but his tired fingers stumbled on the strings and his servants were soon hovering to help him to bed. Once again Kerish let himself be undressed and rubbed with Dirian sponges soaked in perfumed oils. Then at last he was lying in his own bed, curled up beneath the coverlet, staring at the tapestry he had loved since childhood, which showed the Gentle God hand in hand with his Imarko. The servants fastened the shutters, doused the lamps and withdrew to the outer rooms, where they would sleep.

There was no peace in the Prince's dreams. He found himself back in the great hall of the temple. It was night. The place was filled with menacing shadows and he could find no way out. Then the wooden zeloka unfolded its gold and purple wings and flew at him. Kerish dodged the sharp claws of the bird of Truth and ran. There was no escape. The alabaster walls were smooth and relentless and the voice of Ka-Metranee echoed round the hall: "A curse on Golden Galkis!"

Chapter 6

The Book of the Emperors: *Love*
"And I say to you, beware, for those we love best we cannot know. Love clouds our sight and you, my brother, I cannot save."
With these words he departed and they did not meet again.

As soon as the Prince woke and dressed, the routine which had dominated his life for the past nine years began again. His day was divided among the tutors who instructed him in poetry and calligraphy, High Galkian and Zindaric, music and mathematics. Most important of all were the priests whom Kerish visited to learn and recite from the Book of the Emperors and to be taught the history of Galkis and the holy laws of Zeldin.

It was while he sat with them at noon, discussing the meditations of the Silent Emperor, that Kerish heard the trumpets for the entry into Galkis of the High Priest and Prince Im-lo-Torim.

Three hours later the Imperial Summons came. Kerish was sitting cross-legged strumming at his zildar and trying to compose a tune for a poem written by the Crown Prince's primary wife, Kelinda of Seld.

> *My soul is a white bird,*　　*Blown by the east wind*
> *From my heart's home,*　　*Seld, the green and golden*
> *Fair land that I look on*　　*Only in dreams.*
> *And wake, weeping . . .*

Resplendent in a purple fleece and carrying a rod of cirge, an Imperial herald strode into the room. He bowed to Kerish and touched him with the shining rod.

"His Divine Majesty, the Emperor Ka-Litraan, summons thee, Prince Kerish-lo-Taan, to attend his royal presence."

Kerish rose to his feet. "Where must I go?"

"To the Hidden Pavilion," answered the herald. "I will escort your Highness to the gate of the Emperor's gardens."

As Kerish-lo-Taan walked behind the herald through the winding passages of the Inner Palace, he tried to remember when he had last spoken to his father. He had seen the Emperor less than a month ago when he had presided over the ceremony to welcome spring, but that had been a purely formal occasion and they had not spoken. It would have been nearly a year ago, Kerish decided. He had been walking deep in the gardens and had met his father by chance. Even then the Emperor had done no more than murmur that he was growing to be more like his mother.

The herald stopped before a high wall of glassy green brick that curled away to right and left and was pierced by a single gate.

"I will leave your Highness here, for I have a second royal command to execute."

He bowed deeply and strode away. The gate swung open at a touch and Kerish entered the Emperor's garden.

Only once, just before his ninth birthday, had he been to the Hidden Pavilion, but his memories of the way had never faded. The Prince followed narrow paths that constantly twisted and forked, crossed slender bridges over deep pools or gushing streams, and passed under archways embraced by clinging blossoms. As he went deeper in he could not resist stopping occasionally to look or touch, for the gardens of Galkis were justly famed as one of the wonders of Zindar.

If the Golden City was decaying and the Empire threatened, the gardens were more glorious than ever. The Emperor Ka-Litraan had emptied his treasury to buy red rock-inliss from Gannoth, spice trees from distant Kolgor and speckled flowers from the pleasure gardens of Losh. From the land of Four Rivers had come sultry marsh lilies; from Erandachu the windflowers that carpeted the land every spring; from Gilaz spike palms, cruel and sharp to the unwary hand; from Oraz the snake plant whose stems writhed like serpents and whose flowers dripped poison;

and from Seld the crown trees whose yellow blossoms were strewn before queens.

Huge tengis birds, bright feathered and long tailed, strutted on the grass and jewel-like vilic birds, the length of Kerish's little finger, sucked nectar from clumps of azure heaven-flowers. Flights of gaudy butterflies shimmered in the afternoon heat and in dim, green pools swam gold-scaled sun fish from Jenoza and sharp-toothed kirgass from Mintaz.

Kerish wandered through a silvery grove that showered him with white blossoms. He passed by a black pool blotched with red lilies and overhung by the delicate trees that weep for the Poet Emperor and his love. He crossed a slender, high-arched bridge that led to an avenue of dark and ancient illuga. Beyond lay a lawn dotted with tiny gold buds that opened only at sunset, and a wall of fire trees whose scarlet blossoms raged at the wind.

Kerish walked between two trees, taking great care that the flowers on the lowest branches did not touch and burn him. Even he had to stoop slightly to enter the silver door that confronted him. The Hidden Pavilion was carved from translucent crystal and men said it was the work of Zeldin himself. Inside the pavilion the Emperor Ka-Litraan spent all the hours he could spare and many that he could not.

It was here that his rare and cherished orchids were kept and it was stiflingly hot. Between dense banks of brilliant flowers sat the High Priest, who smiled encouragingly at Kerish but did not speak. In the centre of the crystal pavilion grew a glossy-leaved plant, taller than a man. Kerish knew it for the Lord of Flowers, the Emperor orchid, whose huge purple blooms appeared only once in the lifetime of the Godborn.

Beside the orchid, his hands resting on one delicate leaf, stood the Emperor Ka-Litraan. Kerish knelt and then lay face downwards, waiting for royal permission to rise and look at the Emperor's face.

Instead, his father leaned down and raised Kerish up with his own hands. For a moment they looked at each other.

The Emperor's age would have been difficult to guess. His long, raven hair was threaded with white and the veins stood out, blue and hard, on his thin hands, yet his coldly beautiful face was serene, unmarred by the scars of age. Kerish's own face was an almost exact copy and their eyes might have been carved out of one piece of amethyst and inlaid with gold and ebony by the same craftsman. The High Priest watched them, knowing that it was not himself that the Emperor saw mirrored there but a girl who had died sixteen years before.

The Emperor and the High Priest had discussed many things in their brief time together and Izeldon had described the events of the ceremony of Presentation. The Emperor had laughed, a bitter sound, without warmth.

"So Zyrindella has defied our gentle Zeldin once too often. I thought she would."

"You knew . . ."

"Of her deceit, her ambition, her cruelty? Oh, I have watched her closely. I could name every one of her lovers, even the father of her child. I will uphold your sentence of banishment and even give the Governorship of Morolk into other hands but when I am dead, dear uncle, she will find a means to take revenge. She may make that son of hers Emperor yet."

"You are smiling!"

"I smile because the Godborn are not worthy of tears. Don't look at me so, Izeldon. I know that I am the least worthy of all. I will smile at darkness, because we deserve our doom."

"And Kerish? Does he deserve it too?"

"You are going to ask me again to send him away?"

"Yes," the High Priest had answered steadily, and this time the Emperor had listened.

"Look, child," said the Emperor Ka-Litraan, "the Emperor orchid is in bud; it will flower within six or seven days."

Kerish stared hard at the plant, his face totally lacking expression.

"Your son dislikes being called a child," murmured Izeldon.

The Emperor took Kerish's face between his hands and studied him again.

"How old are you now?"

"Eighteen, your Majesty, almost."

"So, Kerish-lo-Taan," the Emperor released him. "You are almost of age and today we must decide your future. But first, pour us some nectar."

Looking around, Kerish saw a crystal flagon of pale liquid and three goblets standing on a small table. He filled two goblets and knelt to offer them to the Emperor and the High Priest.

"And a third for yourself," said Ka-Litraan, "for I think your temper needs a little sweetening."

Kerish smiled ruefully.

"Good," murmured the Emperor, "it pleases me to see you smile, there is time enough for your face to harden into a true mask."

The Emperor, a crystal goblet in his hands, wandered among his orchids and the flowers seemed to lean towards him as he passed.

"You may sit, Kerish, you are pale. You look as if you fled some terror down the hours of darkness."

"I dreamed that the bird of Truth flew at me, your Majesty, and I could not escape."

Ka-Litraan shuddered. "You will never escape that dream until you face truth as I have done." The Emperor stopped to touch an orchid the colour of blood spattered on sand. "Then perhaps you will learn to admire only plants and beasts, who do not love or lie, and kill in innocence."

"Truth may be as beautiful as it is terrible," said the High Priest quietly.

The Emperor laughed. "What, uncle, can nothing bring you to final despair?"

"No," answered Izeldon. "Majesty, remember why we three are together."

The Emperor nodded. "Prince of the Godborn, you will soon be of age. I shall draw one pattern of your future life and the High Priest another. You must choose."

The sun blazed down through the crystal roof; beads of perspiration glittered on Kerish's face and his silk tunic clung damply to his body.

"It is the custom," continued the Emperor, "for the Princes and Lords of the Godborn to be given a city or province to govern. The Crown Prince has dominion over Galkis itself, Ka-Metranee and Im-lo-Torim rule in Holy Hildimarn and Jerenac governs Jenoza. In Morolk my poor nephew and his wife will still rule in name but Zyrindella will be confined to her palace and a worthy regent shall govern in her place. You approve, uncle?"

"I approve, though I fear that you see further than I do."

"It is the Emperor's privilege," said Ka-Litraan bitterly, "and I know my dear children only too well. So we come to Tryfania and Zyrindella's stepfather. He hates me, and with good cause, but he thinks I will repay my guilt by letting one of his sons be Governor after him. He is wrong. I intend Tryfania for you, Kerish-lo-Taan, but not just yet. You need more experience, and the Governor of Ephaan is an old man with one young daughter.

"If you choose, you shall govern our port of Ephaan and marry Selona, the old Lord's daughter. In perhaps five years' time you will also marry the youngest daughter of the Governor of Tryfania and replace him in Trykis. You may, if you choose, appoint Yxin, your future brother by marriage, as Governor of Far Tryfarn. It might pacify him, but do not underrate the danger of his allying with Zyrindella against you. Well, Kerish, will you stay in Galkis and begin by governing Ephaan, or will you throw your life away for a glimmering hope? No, don't answer yet, let the High Priest speak."

The High Priest rose and bowed to the Emperor. "I have spoken to you, Kerish, of a quest for a Saviour who can restore the harmony of heaven to our troubled land. In wisdom he shall excel all the Lords of the Godborn and he will bind together the divided peoples of our Empire."

"Empires fall and Emperors die," said Ka-Litraan. "Glory fades and greatness is forgotten. That is the way of men. Let darkness come to the Godborn, Izeldon."

"If the Saviour is not freed," answered the High Priest,

"then darkness will cover all our sins. Even if He comes you and I will not live to see it."

"No, there will be no light in my darkness," murmured the Emperor, "and if he chooses this quest I shall not see my son again."

"Father!" The word came unthinkingly to Kerish's lips. "Father, I will do whatever you ask. If you want me to stay . . ."

"No." It was almost a shout but the Emperor's hand touched Kerish's cheek as gently as he might have caressed a half-opened flower.

"Uncle, pay your Emperor no attention, you must speak on."

It was the High Priest's turn to pace between the banks of flowers, his hands folded inside the breast of his robe.

"Majesty, Highness, no man in Zindar knows where the prison of the Saviour stands."

"It is not written in the Book of Secrets," affirmed the Emperor, "yet we are told to seek knowledge from the first High Priest and the last."

From inside his robe, Izeldon drew out a chain of cirge but his cupped hands hid whatever hung from it.

"Ask," he said, "and I will answer."

The High Priest's eyes were still open but they were like a blind man's, dull and unfocused.

"Or looking inwards," thought Kerish.

"Tongue of Zeldin," cried the Emperor, "it is time. We seek the Saviour of Galkis. Speak!"

There was a long silence, as if the High Priest was struggling to recover something from the deep of memory. When he began to speak, it was very softly. Kerish strained to hear and at first the language seemed alien. It was High Galkian but the words were distorted into strange, new shapes.

"No, not new," Kerish realized, "ancient shapes."

For the first time he saw language as a living thing, spreading across the centuries, growing, changing; and this was a voice from the childhood of Galkian.

"Seven gates and seven locks, but I am the key, a key of flesh and a key of spirit in each generation. Child of the

Godborn, seven keys must you win, keys of gold, keys of death."

As Kerish watched, the High Priest's hands whitened until his skin was almost translucent, and his bones were like the bars of a cage of light.

"Seven cold keys but the last and the first are keys of flesh and spirit."

"Where?" demanded the Emperor. "Where must he seek?"

"Where there is least safety and most hope." The High Priest's body rocked and his voice soared. "Seven citadels must you breach; seven sorcerers must you conquer; seven keys to the last gates. Seek the Enchanter King; seek the Tyrant of Ellerinonn!"

Light seemed to break from the High Priest's hands and surge towards Kerish. For a moment he wondered why he had not noticed the darkness of the day before that light. Then it was gone.

"Child of the Godborn," Izeldon's voice rang through the Hidden Pavilion, "receive the token that you shall bear to Ellerinonn. Receive what you cannot accept!"

Gently the Emperor pushed his son forward. Kerish knelt and the High Priest opened his hands, snatching off the glittering chain to hang it round the Prince's neck.

"It is gone," murmured Izeldon, "and without the burden I have no strength."

The High Priest crumpled but the Emperor sprang from his chair and caught him as he fell.

"The nectar, quickly, Kerish."

The Prince hastily poured out another cup and knelt to press it to Izeldon's lips. The High Priest's eyes fluttered open. For a moment they were as blank as a mirror facing nothingness, then Kerish knew that Izeldon saw him again.

"Child," he whispered, "Kerish, forgive me."

Izeldon's face seemed taut enough to break into a thousand fissures.

"He is old, so old," thought Kerish.

"Drink, uncle," chided the Emperor, "there is more to do before you can rest."

The High Priest swallowed obediently and Ka-Litraan lifted the old man with surprising ease and placed him on his chair. As Kerish stood up, something cold and hard swung against his chest and he squinted down at it. A purple gem with a heart of white fire hung from the chain.

"You wear the Jewel of Zeldin," said the Emperor. "Nine chapters of the Book of Secrets do not suffice to describe it, but it has no worth unless you can discover its virtues for yourself."

"But the Seven Sorcerers . . ." began Kerish.

"Ah, the Book speaks also of their long search for knowledge . . . Immortality was the reward of their compact with Zeldin. Yet even I do not know where all their citadels stand," admitted the Emperor. "Elmandis rules fair Ellerinonn. A second sorcerer lives on the Isle of Cheransee and is a terror to all ships that pass through the Straits of Rac. In the Red Waste, in the Kingdom of Seld, there is a third whose citadel is a place of dread. Of the rest I can tell you nothing. They have withdrawn from the world."

"But King Elmandis will know!" declared Kerish. "I will seek him in Ellerinonn."

Izeldon sat upright again, though when he spoke his voice was very tired.

"You are resolved, then, to search for the keys to our Saviour's prison?"

"Yes," cried Kerish. "How could I bear to stay mewed up in Galkis when you have shown me what my life could be? Yes, yes."

"You would go beyond the shadow of the Godborn?" asked the Emperor.

"Yes, my Lord, if I have your blessing."

The Emperor stretched out a thin hand, but this time he did not touch his son.

"You have my blessing, but you cannot go alone."

Sound shivered through the crystal pavilion as the royal herald struck the door with his rod of cirge.

"Kerish, I have sent for your half-brother," said the Emperor. "Bid him enter."

Kerish hurried to the doorway where Forollkin stood,

looking curiously about him. He had always kept to the fringes of the garden before for he did not know the paths and had been warned of the dangers mingled with the beauty.

Kerish dismissed the herald, and Forollkin cast himself down to make the seven proscribed obeisances. The Emperor coldly ordered him to rise. Forollkin looked at the Emperor of Galkis, at the Prince standing by his side and at the pale figure of Izeldon. He sensed an affinity between them that he could never share, no matter how close he was to Kerish.

"It is known to me," began Ka-Litraan, "that you wish to go with my Lord Commander to Jenoza and serve him as chief Captain."

Forollkin was silent, wondering how the Emperor knew.

"Is this not so?"

"Yes, Majesty," said Forollkin.

Kerish would have spoken but Izeldon laid a warning hand on his wrist.

"Lord Forollkin," began the Emperor, "for five years you have been a Captain in the Imperial Guard, and the chosen companion of my royal son. Does this life no longer please you?"

"No, Majesty," answered Forollkin bravely.

"Why is this?" enquired the Emperor. "Is it because of the new scar on your cheek? If so, my son shall pay you blood fee. You, yourself, shall draw the dagger across his face, scar for scar. He will submit, I promise you."

"No!" exclaimed Forollkin. "No, I couldn't!"

"Your anger, then, is dead?"

"Yes, Majesty."

"Well we must seek elsewhere for the causes of your discontent."

The Emperor sat down, leaving his sons to stand facing one another.

"Perhaps Forollkin will name them himself," said Izeldon gently.

"Speak freely then," commanded Ka-Litraan.

"Your Majesty, your Holiness," began Forollkin, "I

77

was trained as a soldier but the Inner Palace is no place for swords. It is beautiful, but it chokes me. I am no courtier, and there is so much here that I could never understand. Let me serve you with my body, to guard Jenoza or to fight against the Brigands of Fangmere. Let me do what I know I can do, away from, from..." Forollkin faltered but the Emperor said calmly, "You desire action, danger, freedom?"

"Yes, Majesty."

"Forollkin, I may send you into even greater danger than you desire," murmured the Emperor. "Do you know why I chose you as a companion for Prince Kerish-lo-Taan? It was for your faults. They are the mirror to your brother's virtues and his failings are checked by the wall of your strengths. I am glad when you quarrel, for it confirms your differences but you should not separate. Together you may achieve much, apart, very little. For the sake of Galkis you must not be divided, and I wish you to swear that you will never leave Kerish unless he commands it. As your Emperor I could order you to do this. Instead, I beg you."

Ka-Litraan held out his hand to Forollkin and touched him for the first time in their lives.

"Majesty, I..." The young captain looked helplessly from Izeldon's calm face to Kerish's imploring eyes. "I swear it," he said desperately. "I won't leave Kerish."

"The Emperor of the Godborn witnesses your oath," pronounced Ka-Litraan, "and if in the long night of eternity you break it, may the bird of Truth devour your soul."

After a moment's silence, Kerish said, "Majesty, may I tell him now?"

"Surely," answered the Emperor, with a curious half-smile. "Does not the Book of the Emperors say that obedience without knowledge shall have a fitting reward?"

"Forollkin, I have been chosen to search for the promised Saviour and you are to come with me. The Seven Sorcerers hold the keys to his prison and we must persuade them to give the keys up. First the Enchanter King of Ellerinonn..."

As Kerish spilled out his news, Forollkin gradually caught his half-brother's excitement.

"You mean we are to be trusted with all this? Kerish, why didn't you tell me?"

"Because I forbade it," said the High Priest quietly, and Forollkin suddenly remembered in whose company he stood.

"Forollkin," said the Emperor, "this is a journey that will take you far from Palace and Empire, to lands where the Godborn are not honoured. You will have to make your own respect. There will be difficulties and dangers and to protect your brother will take all the skill and courage you have. Are you resolved to go?"

"Yes, Majesty," answered Forollkin steadily.

"Then you, Kerish, will shortly be proclaimed Governor of Ephaan," announced the Emperor. "Forollkin will accompany you as military Commander and you will travel in state. I shall, however, send letters to the present Governor of Ephaan ordering him to fit out a ship for your voyage to Ellerinonn. You will be long gone from Galkis before anyone in the Palace guesses your absence. Will this serve, uncle?"

"Most well," exclaimed Izeldon.

The Emperor smiled in bitter acknowledgment. "I should rather have been the last Lord of the Godborn, but I will play my part in Zeldin's dance. Kerish, lead your half-brother back through the gardens. You must hurry if you are to attend the Name Feast of our dear Queen."

"Yes, Majesty." Kerish and Forollkin began their parting obeisances but the Emperor stooped to whisper to them: "Feast then, but never drink from a crimson cup, for crimson is the colour of death."

When his sons had gone, the Emperor murmured, "There is perhaps one thing I should have told them."

"This once, spare me your knowledge." The High Priest's voice cracked as he spoke.

"I will spare you," said Ka-Litraan, "but uncle, how often have you accused me of letting Galkis slide into darkness? You cannot know what I have done and suffered today to save her."

Chapter 7

The Book of the Emperors: *Sorrows*
And the Godborn must look into the eyes of death and smile,
for death is the gift of Zeldin to men.

As they walked back together through the gardens, Forollkin started to plan.

"A state journey along the Royal Road would take an age, but you need not travel by litter all the way. No, we will take good horses and use them once we are well clear of the city. We should reach Ephaan just when the seas are calmest."

Forollkin went on to talk about their escort and what baggage they should take. Kerish stopped listening. He should have realized that Forollkin would take over the leadership of the expedition, but *he* was the one that the High Priest had chosen, that must not be forgotten.

"What will you tell your mother?" asked Kerish suddenly.

Forollkin halted in the middle of a list of necessary provisions and thought for a moment.

"Just that the Emperor has ordered me to go with you to Ephaan as Commander. She can't expect me to refuse an Imperial order."

"Be careful, you were never good at lying."

"No, that's another royal talent that I lack."

"Well guard your tongue, or your mother will drag the truth past it," said Kerish.

"What do you know about mothers?" retorted Forollkin. "You don't even remember yours."

Even so, he knew that the Prince was right, and was on his guard when he entered his mother's pavilion.

Follea was already dressed for the banquet. One of her slaves was holding up a mirror, while another fastened gold pins in the thick braids of her hair. Before Forollkin could speak, she snapped: "Where have you been this last hour? Lord Jerenac has had men searching for you all over the Palace."

"The Emperor sent for me."

Follea studied his face, reflected in the copper mirror. "And what did the Emperor of Galkis, may his reign be eternal, have to say to his son?"

Forollkin stood as stiffly as if he were talking to his Commander. "I have been ordered to accompany Prince Kerish-lo-Taan to Ephaan. I am to be in charge of the city's defences and the Prince is to be Governor."

Follea dismissed her slaves and then asked: "Did the Emperor know of Lord Jerenac's plans for you?"

"He knew," answered Forollkin steadily, "and he made it clear that I would not do well to accept Jerenac's favours."

"But Jerenac holds Viroc, he is the strongest Lord in Galkis," protested Follea.

"Mother, if the Emperor chose to destroy the Lord Commander I believe he could do it at a word. He masks his power, but he is Emperor still."

"But for how long?" Follea fastened an amber necklace about her throat. "It is said that the claws of death have marked his face at last, and death must follow."

"It is a false rumour," said Forollkin.

Follea considered. "Well, perhaps you are fortunate. Jerenac's pride and plain speech may trip him yet. If only you would pay court to the Crown Prince or the Lady Gankali . . . but of all sons you are the least likely to bring your mother fortune and glory."

"Mother," Forollkin put his hands on her shoulder. "Mother, you should be glad. Ephaan is a great city and I shall command all her defences, the fleet too. Would you care for a son who was Lord Admiral of Galkis?"

"The sea is fickle, and a drowned son will not protect me in my darkening years."

"Mother, you are loved and honoured here!"

"But Forollkin," Follea reached up to smooth her son's brown hair, "how could I bear to live so far apart from my only child? When you are settled in copper-walled Ephaan, you shall send for me."

Not knowing what to say, Forollkin laughed and kissed her.

Follea pushed him away. "I must attend the Queen and help her robe for the Feast. See you are dressed in time, and fittingly, no slouching about in worn tunic and dusty cloak."

"No, Mother," said Forollkin meekly.

"Remember, half the court will be there and the Ambassador of Oraz."

"Of Oraz? I hadn't heard," Forollkin frowned.

"He arrived two days ago, a fierce black-bearded barbarian, just what you would expect. The Emperor has not given him an audience yet and I don't believe he will. That duty will fall to the Crown Prince."

Follea picked up an ivory-handled fan and smoothed her silken skirts. "You had better send your apologies to Lord Jerenac; never slam a door you may still need to walk through!"

Forollkin bowed his head and did not look up until she had gone.

He tried to imagine Follea's reaction when she heard that her son had sailed off on some wild quest with Prince Kerish. He knew there would be more anger in it than grief. In the past few years Follea had tried to bind her son to her with chains of duty and affection but she had left him too long in the care of the Palace slaves. Until he was fifteen she had rarely seen or spoken to him. All Forollkin could feel at their parting was a dogged sense of guilt.

Reluctantly he turned his mind to the coming banquet. Returning to his quarters, Forollkin bathed and changed into his most splendid and uncomfortable clothes. His body servant helped him on with his gilded boots and declared that he would outbrave all the young Lords of Galkis. Forollkin, who was far happier in his shabby riding clothes, snorted contemptuously and strode off across the courtyard.

To the despair of his servants, Prince Kerish-lo-Taan had not started to prepare for the feast until half an hour before it was due to start. Then he had thrown on a tunic of blue silk, stiff with silver embroidery, and let them comb out his hair and crown him with cirge.

Forollkin waited as Kerish hurriedly clasped a bracelet of cabochon garnets about his slim wrist. As usual, Forollkin exclaimed:

"Zeldin's mercy, aren't you ready yet?"

Kerish smiled at him hopefully. "Truly I'm ready."

"You intend to go barefoot then?"

"Oh." Kerish snatched up his jewelled sandals and put them on.

Torch–bearers arrived but Kerish waved away the waiting litter and walked by Forollkin's side through a series of splendid courtyards.

"The Ambassador of Oraz will be at the banquet tonight," whispered Forollkin. "Can you guess why he's come?"

"To announce the new alliance formally I suppose, and informally to threaten us."

"What will the Emperor do?" asked Forollkin.

"Laugh," answered Kerish.

Beneath a roof spanned by carved and gilded zelokas, on a dais draped with purple silk, ten ivory thrones had been set around an ebony table. Below the dais were more tables for those guests privileged to look on the unveiled faces of the Godborn, but in the centre of the hall was a space in which the Palace actors would later perform. The lower tables that would once have been filled with men and women ennobled by their craft or learning were now crowded with idle gentry, brilliant in the robes of their hereditary offices; and court ladies, laughing behind gauzy veils, their braided hair piled fantastically on their heads.

When the trumpets sounded for the entry of the Godborn the company rose from their seats, the men bowing and the ladies sweeping low curtsies. In slow and splendid procession the Royal Kindred entered the Great Hall but it did not go unnoticed by the guests that Zyrindella and her husband were absent and that neither the

Emperor nor the High Priest had chosen to honour the Queen's Name Feast.

To Forollkin's surprise he was seated at the High Table next to Jerenac and Yxin who had returned from the temple together that morning. The Lord Commander gave him a penetrating look but as yet they had had no chance to speak. On either side of the central throne sat the sons of Queen Rimoka, Im-lo-Torim and Ka-Rim-Loka. Beside the Crown Prince were his two wives, Gankali and the Princess Kelinda of Seld. Beyond her sat Kerish and, rather to his alarm, the throne next to him was left vacant for the Ambassador of Oraz.

The trumpets blared again for the entry of Queen Rimoka. The barbarian Princess of Chiraz had outlived the Emperor's other two wives and borne his heir. Now she wore the wealth of Galkis like armour to defend her vanishing beauty. Rimoka was tall and gaunt. In a lean face, close-set, black eyes gleamed on either side of a hooked nose. Her iron-grey hair was woven with gems and her robe was so richly embroidered that it was impossible to guess the colour of the cloth beneath. Follea carried her train and twelve noble ladies followed humbly behind.

As the Queen reached the dais, each of the Godborn knelt to kiss the hem of her robe. Kerish seemed to crouch at her feet for an age while the company stared and whispered, before Rimoka gave him permission to rise. The Queen of Galkis seated herself on the central throne and Follea and her ladies withdrew to the nearest of the lesser tables.

"Give entrance to the Lord Ambassador of Oraz," commanded Rimoka.

No trumpets sounded, the courtiers stood at their places and the Ambassador stepped into a gaping silence.

Kerish and Forollkin both studied the Ambassador intently as he walked slowly and majestically through the hall. He was a huge man, taller than any of the Godborn, broad-shouldered and thickly made. A mane of black hair and a flowing beard framed his heavy-jowled face. He was dressed in bronze mail and a cloak and buskins made from the skin of one of the great green serpents of Oraz. As an ambassador he must carry no weapons, but his massive hands could have squeezed the life out of any Galkian. Kerish guessed his name before the herald announced it: O-grak the Strong, Khan of Orze and uncle to the Prince of Oraz.

He saluted the Queen in the fashion of the Five Kingdoms, his right arm across his breast. Rimoka spoke to him in Zindaric.

"My Lord Ambassador, in the name of Zeldin the Peaceful, you are welcome to Galkis. By the Grace of the Emperor, may his reign be eternal, you shall sit tonight among the Godborn and no one shall offer you injury."

"Gracious Queen, Princes, Lords and Ladies of the Godborn," the Ambassador's voice boomed through the hall, "in the name of the Dark Goddess I thank you for your welcome, and for your assurance of my safety. Your words still my fears as water douses fire."

O-grak saluted everyone at the high table in turn and then took his place beside Kerish.

The company at the lower tables could at last sit down but the feast would not begin until the naming of Queen Rimoka had been properly celebrated. The trumpets sounded once for every year of her life and the chief of the royal poets stepped forward to chant a long poem in her praise. It was dull and spiritless and Rimoka sat through it with a contemptuous smile, but the nobles schooled their faces to appear enthralled.

As the poet droned on, Khan O-grak turned to Kerish and whispered loudly, "What does this poet sing about, Prince?"

"It is a chant in the ancient tongue in praise of Queen Rimoka," Kerish whispered back.

"Hah, in Oraz I would slit the throat of any poet who sang my praises with so little fire in his voice."

"It is not the custom . . ." Kerish broke off as Rimoka turned her steely gaze on them.

When the chant was over the Queen threw the poet a silver ring and the rest of the Godborn had to outmatch her generosity by tossing down coins and jewels. O-grak fingered a golden table knife.

85

"For my gift he would have this through his heart but I fancy the Queen would be displeased."

Kerish tried hard not to smile. "Probably, my Lord, but then she has no ear for music."

"No? There is nothing that pleasures me more than a stirring song of high deeds and great battles," declared the Khan.

"I fear you will find our songs pale and dull. They rarely tell of war."

"I know," said O-grak in a hoarse whisper. "You Galkians do not love war as we do. Your Emperors take more joy in the zildar than the sword."

"More joy, yes," answered Kerish quickly, "but we *can* wield the sword and we have other powers far more dangerous to those who threaten us."

"So I have heard, Prince," murmured O-grak, "heard, but not seen."

"Then pray to your Dark Goddess that you never will see it."

"Oh I do, Prince," chuckled the Ambassador, "I do."

As they spoke, servants set before each of the Godborn a cup carved from a single precious stone. The Chief Steward of the Palace bore round a flagon, and filled the cups with precious golden nectar. Rising to their feet the Godborn drank to long life and joy for Queen Rimoka. The jewel cups flashed in the torchlight, blue and green, yellow and red. The Queen bowed her head in acknowledgement and the banquet began.

Forollkin helped himself to a haunch of meat stuck with cloves but before he could bite into it Lord Jerenac leaned towards him: "Boy," he said gruffly, "you are harder to find than a pearl in a snowdrift. Where have you been?"

"The Emperor summoned me," answered Forollkin.

"Small wonder you've kept silent then, but I'll have your answer now," barked Jerenac, oblivious to the interested glances of Yxin and the Queen.

"My heart follows you to Jenoza," said Forollkin, "but my body cannot. I am commanded elsewhere by the Emperor."

"What, has your pretty Prince beguiled the Emperor to rob me of you?"

"I do not know," said Forollkin quietly. "My Lord, I am truly sorry that my sword cannot be at your service."

Jerenac nodded. "That I'll believe. Well, the Captaincy must go to another but if you win free of this new destiny, come to me and you'll find a welcome."

"Thank you." Forollkin was too moved to say more.

Jerenac turned away to speak to Yxin, and with diminished appetite Forollkin began his meal.

Nothing, however, disturbed the appetite of Prince Imlo-Torim. The Priest Governor of Hildimarn had already collected a large array of dishes and set them out in front of him. He began with slices of iced fruit, cold enough to numb the mouth, and went on to a bowl of scalding pepper soup. Next, the Prince consumed three sweet young birds, roasted and stuffed with nuts, a dish of spiced kardiss and a mound of sickly cakes drowned in a heavy syrup. To take away the sweetness he ate three sour cereets and then looked about for something new to shock his palate.

While his brother immersed himself in the pleasures of food the Crown Prince listened contentedly to the chatter of his wife Gankali. Tonight she was gaudier than ever in a blaze of jewels and red silk. Li-Kroch had once compared her to a Jenozan parrot and it was apt. She was as brightly coloured as any jungle bird and her constant chatter as witless.

Princess Kelinda also tried once to speak to her husband but he did not hear, or if he did, chose to ignore her. With gentle dignity, Kelinda turned instead to Kerish. Beside Gankali's vulgar splendour the Princess of Seld with her plain gown and neat braids of pale copper hair seemed more shadowy than ever. Yet when she spoke her voice was startlingly low and rich and her grey eyes, suffused with thought, could compel her listeners' attention.

"Have you finished setting that poem of mine, Kerish?"

The Ambassador was busy tearing at a haunch of meat and washing it down with the strongest wine, so Kerish felt free to talk. "Not yet. I haven't been in a sad enough mood."

"Ah, you must forgive my melancholy, but while I was walking in the Emperor's garden I came across a grove of crown trees." Kelinda sighed. "They are like the trees I saw every morning from my window on Trykis. They brought back memories of other springs."

Kerish sensed something of her loneliness. "If the crown trees can grow and flourish in Galkis, then so can you."

"Well, at least I have grown to love your gardens," admitted Kelinda.

"And when the sky is clear, I love the sight of the Holy Mountain overawing the city, and most of all I love the statue of Imarko in her temple here; beautiful as any goddess and yet so human."

"Our Lady kept her humanity for our sake," said Kerish.

Kelinda nodded gravely. "And she died for you too. Perhaps we should not speak of these things on such an occasion. Forgive me if I have not learned all of your customs yet."

"You learn about Galkis far faster than you can teach me about Seld," said Kerish. "I lag far behind you."

"I learn from necessity, you from pleasure," answered Kelinda with a sad smile.

"My curiosity may be of more use that I expected," said Kerish but ignoring Kelinda's questioning look he went on to ask her if she had any new manuscripts from Seld that he could try to read. The Princess described the scrolls that had recently arrived with a courier from Ephaan, and they were soon deep in a discussion of the respective merits of two Seldian poetesses.

Under the cold gaze of Queen Rimoka the conversation at the lower tables had been subdued, but as the wine was passed round bursts of laughter and snatches of song floated up to the dais. The women began to lift their gauzy veils and the men to talk and argue more forcibly. On the high table Gankali, flushes breaking through her carefully whitened cheeks, leaned closer to her husband, whispering and giggling. Im-lo-Torim continued to gorge himself while his mother expertly questioned the Lord Commander on the defences of Viroc. Suddenly Yxin broke in on them.

"Pardon me, your Majesty, but since you are talking of

battles and barbarians, has your Majesty asked our good Lord Forollkin where he got his new scar?"

"What are you prattling about, Yxin?" snapped Rimoka but the flicker of her dark eyes towards Forollkin betrayed her interest.

"Prince Kerish-lo-Taan rashly challenged me to a duel with Tryfanian whips," said Yxin. "Of course within minutes I had beaten him and had him at my mercy, though I took care not to hurt him. He is my kinsman."

"Sit still," whispered Kelinda urgently, gripping Kerish by the wrist. "Never let them see that you care."

Rimoka was laughing and telling Yxin to go on.

"So," he continued, "having failed against me, our Prince vented his spite on poor Forollkin and slashed him across the face with a whip!"

"A vicious trick," said Rimoka, "but then his mother had a temper as wild as an unbroken Irollga."

Everyone at the high table was now listening but, with Kelinda still clutching his wrist, Kerish spoke calmly.

"Lord Yxin does not tell the whole story, Majesty. He does not say how he basely insulted Lord Forollkin and then refused to fight with him, because he did not dare."

"You lie," shouted Yxin.

Heads turned at the lower tables and conversation faltered.

"Forollkin," said Rimoka, "you are silent. What do you have to say to this?"

"What the Prince says is true," replied Forollkin quietly. "Lord Yxin insulted me and then refused to fight me because I am the son of a concubine. Prince Kerish-lo-Taan fought gallantly in my stead. As to my scar . . . Yxin was half-way out of the courtyard. He could not have seen what happened. It was an accident."

Kerish stared at his brother. It was the first time he had ever heard him tell a direct lie.

"Yxin, you had better cease your boasting," growled Jerenac. "If you and Forollkin were matched with swords I know who would be the winner, even though he is the son of a concubine . . . like myself."

"I meant no offence to you, my Lord," said Yxin hastily,

"and I honour Lord Forollkin for lying to protect his master. After all the Prince is too young to be held responsible."

"But not too young to be appointed Lord Governor of Ephaan," said Kerish quietly.

Every head at the table turned to look at him.

"You are jesting, Prince," suggested Rimoka.

"No, your Majesty. I leave for Ephaan in six days time, and Lord Forollkin is to accompany me."

"Kerish," whispered Kelinda, "and you never thought to tell me!"

"I did not know myself until today," said the Prince hastily.

"The Emperor must have sold his wits to the wind to send a child to govern Ephaan," began Rimoka, "but then he was always bewitched by . . ."

"No doubt the Emperor was advised by his Holiness," interrupted Im-lo-Torim.

"No doubt, my dear," Rimoka checked her anger. "Well, we must wish you Zeldin's favour in your new appointment, Kerish. I fear that one so young and with so little experience of the world may need it."

Kerish answered with quiet dignity: "I thank you for your gentle wishes, and I have faith in Zeldin's mercy."

"Such piety is most commendable," said Rimoka flatly, "and we must pledge your health."

The Godborn rose, Gankali leaning unsteadily against her husband, and drank to the new Governor of Ephaan.

"Now, let the temple actors begin," commanded Rimoka.

O-grak turned to Kerish. "My congratulations, Prince. Ephaan is a fair city, if hard to defend."

"Lord Forollkin will be military commander," answered Kerish, "and no doubt he has plans to strengthen the defences, for these are troubled times."

"Indeed, indeed, for I know you are plagued in the north by the Brigands of Fangmere."

"A few paltry raids," said Kerish, sipping at his wine.

"I hear also," continued the Ambassador, "that the Jorgan Isles are now so infested with the ships of Fangmere that the passage of the Sea of Az is safe for no vessel."

"I will take your word on it," replied Kerish. "The Ambassador of Oraz should certainly know the movements of the fleet of Fangmere."

O-grak duly noted that rumours of the alliance between the Five Kingdoms and the men of Fangmere had reached Galkis and changed the subject.

"A pretty ornament, Prince." He took Kerish's wrist and examined the silver and red bracelet. "My new wife would walk barefoot over swords for such a jewel as this."

Kerish at once unfastened the bracelet and gave it to O-grak.

"She shall win it at a word," he said, and smiled.

The Ambassador stared at him for a moment. "You are generous, Prince."

"It is nothing," answered Kerish carelessly. "The wealth of Galkis can pay a dozen armies as easily as it can spare a bracelet."

O-grak nodded reflectively. "I will remember your words, Prince, when I return to Oraz."

"My Lord Ambassador," Kelinda leaned across the table, her copper hair gleaming in the torchlight, "see the temple actors are about to begin. They are to tell the story of Prince Il-Keno and the Enchantress. Do you know it?"

A smile twitched at the bearded lips. "We have no such dainty tales in Oraz, only legends of war, of bloody vengeance and the slaying of monsters."

"Then we will tell you the story as the action passes. Perhaps you will learn to love our gentle tales."

"I think not, Lady," said the Ambassador of Oraz.

The open space between the lower tables was now filled with brightly clothed actors and dancers. Six musicians sat in a semicircle holding zildars, cymbals, drums and flutes. They began to play a soft, beguiling tune and the high, sweet voice of the chief singer thrilled through the hall. He sang of the glorious reign of the Emperor Ke-no-Kaatan and of his son Il-Keno. The chief of the temple actors entered, robed in purple silk and glittering with false jewels. He wore an ancient ivory mask to represent the face of Prince Il-Keno.

A chorus of Jenozan women sang of their terror of the Enchantress of the Jungle and of the banebirds that were her servants. Kelinda and Kerish whispered explanations to the Ambassador, who nodded and smiled. Prince Il-Keno resolved to enter the Forbidden Jungle of Jenze, though the chorus warned him of its dangers, and to seek out the evil Enchantress. Flutes and zildars played weird, discordant music as the actor mimed his dangerous journey through the jungle. Suddenly twelve dancing banebirds erupted on to the floor. They wore grotesquely carved and painted masks and long, trailing cloaks of scarlet feathers. The banebirds darted at the Prince, shrieking harshly above drumbeats and the clash of cymbals.

Prince Il-Keno raised his hands and cried out to Zeldin for aid. For a moment there was silence and then, from the back of the hall, strode a tall figure in a glorious, golden mask. Kerish's heart leapt as the singer burst into a hymn of praise to the Gentle God. As the golden figure approached the banebirds fell to the ground, heaving and shaking with terror so comically that the Ambassador roared with laughter. The Prince prostrated himself before the god whose hands were raised in blessing.

Kerish's concentration was suddenly broken by a choked cry from someone at the high table. He turned to look just as Gankali slumped forward, retching. A flagon overturned, spilling amber wine. The Crown Prince struggled to his feet and held his wife by the shoulders. Gankali moaned with pain, and vomited a noisome green liquid on to the silken cloth.

Yxin and Jerenac got to their feet and the courtiers at the lower tables noticed the confusion on the dais and were distracted from the performance.

Between spasms Gankali whispered something and the Crown Prince cried hysterically, "Poison. She is poisoned!"

The actors faltered, the golden mask of Zeldin was turned towards the dais and silence crept over the hall.

"Poisoned," repeated the Crown Prince dazedly.

"My son, you forget yourself," hissed Rimoka. She spoke loudly to the company. "Do not be alarmed; sickness is common in the Lady Gankali's happy state."

She turned to the temple actors. "Play on."

Falteringly, the actors spoke their lines and the musicians played again, but all eyes were on the dais.

Her gaudy robes streaked with blood and bile, Gankali was helped from her seat by the Crown Prince and Kelinda. Rimoka spoke calmly to the Ambassador.

"The Princess is far gone with child. No doubt the food and wine have proved too rich for her."

"No doubt, Majesty," growled O-grak.

But before Gankali could be helped from the hall, she gave a wild shriek and broke away from her husband and Kelinda. She staggered a few steps, vomiting blood, and then collapsed. Gankali heaved once and lay still.

Kerish ran to her and knelt. The Crown Prince was already stooping over the sprawled body. Kerish took her wrist and then felt among the spoiled silks for her heartbeat. He drew back a stained hand and whispered, "She is dead."

"No, no." The Crown Prince shook the pathetic body, trying to force life back into it. Conscious of the watching eyes, Kerish said sharply: "Carry her out of the hall. Carry her!"

Obediently the Crown Prince lifted his wife and, staggering under the weight, carried her from the hall.

Kerish took Kelinda's hand and led her back to the high table. His look told Rimoka that her son's wife was dead. But grim-faced she ordered the banquet to continue.

In front of half their court and the Ambassador of Oraz the Godborn must show neither grief nor concern. No one touched the food or wine at the high table as the story of Il-Keno and the Enchantress came to its triumphant conclusion. When the actors had withdrawn O-grak enquired after Gankali.

"She has fainted," answered Kerish.

At midnight Queen Rimoka rose to end the banquet in honour of her name-day. Kerish managed to walk calmly out of the hall and then fled along a corridor into an empty room and was violently sick. Forollkin hurried after him and gripped his shoulders.

"Kerish, you're not . . ."

"No, but Gankali is dead . . . poisoned."

"But how? We all ate much the same food, drank the same wine . . ."

"Crimson is the colour of death," murmured Kerish. "And each of our nectar cups is different."

"You don't think that the Emperor . . ." began Forollkin, appalled, but Kerish said hastily, "No. Yet he knew what was going to happen. He knew."

A servant knocked respectfully and entered.

"Your pardon, Highness, but the Queen and the Lord Commander request Lord Forollkin's attendance."

"Highness, can you spare me?"

Kerish nodded. Forollkin ordered the servant to assemble torch-bearers to escort the Prince back to his apartments and then made his way to the Crown Prince's chambers.

The Queen, Jerenac and Im-lo-Torim were seated at a lacquered table, already discussing Gankali's death as a danger to the reputation of the Godborn, not as a grief. But in a side chamber the Crown Prince sat hunched over his dead wife, stroking her bright hair. Standing at his side, Kelinda tried to comfort him but he did not hear her.

Long after midnight, Kerish's servants tapped timidly at his bedroom door to ask if his half-brother should be admitted. Soon Kerish was fully awake and Forollkin was sitting on the end of his bed, anxious to talk.

"You were right, it was the nectar cup. Im-lo-Torim tested it and thinks the poison was ulgan. It is tasteless and swift, though it has a bitter smell."

"Which the sweet scent of the nectar would have hidden."

"Exactly. I helped Lord Jerenac to question the steward and the four servants who had handled the cups but none of them admitted anything."

"Then how will you find out?" asked Kerish. "The Emperor would know which of them is lying."

"But he has declined to help. Jerenac sent them to the men of his escort for . . . further questioning."

"Do you mean torture?" Kerish sat upright. "But that's barbaric. The Godborn have never used such methods."

"The Godborn have never been murdered before," said Forollkin dryly.

"But some of those men must be innocent. Don't you care?"

"I don't like it," admitted Forollkin, "but I don't see any alternative."

"You'd think differently if you saw it happening."

"Probably I would, but thank Zeldin I don't have your imagination," said Forollkin with a bleak smile.

"So the innocent must suffer for the real murderess!" declared Kerish.

"Yes. Zyrindella's name was never spoken but it was obvious what the Queen was thinking."

"The Emperor will never let her punish Zyrindella."

"He could not," said Forollkin grimly, "not openly, or who would honour the Godborn then?"

"Torturers of the innocent deserve no honour," answered Kerish sullenly.

"Kerish, we cannot always be gentle, or we will lose everything it is our duty to guard. You are still very young and you don't . . ."

"Oh, Imarko have mercy, not you as well!" cried Kerish, "I'm only three years younger than you, that's all and I won't be treated as a child, especially by you!"

He looked so absurdly angry that Forollkin laughed.

"Kerish, I only meant that you've seen so little of the world beyond Palace and temple . . . you're as prickly as a Gilazian spike palm."

"You give me cause," muttered Kerish, "you all do."

"Nonsense," answered Forollkin briskly, "you imagine insults everywhere, thick as thorns, and bleed from your own fancies. Now let me go, Kerish. It's been a long night and I am to be in charge of the funeral escort tomorrow."

Forollkin stretched out a hand to ruffle the Prince's hair but Kerish shrank back. Awkwardly Forollkin withdrew his hand. "Goodnight then."

When he was gone, Kerish's eyes stared fiercely after him.

"I will show you," he thought over and over again. "I will show you on our quest whether I am a child or a man."

Later, just before he fell asleep, he remembered that he had not thanked Forollkin for a lie told before all the Godborn.

Chapter 8

The Book of the Emperors: *Warnings*

*Treat even the lightest parting as though it were the last, as
though you set out, not to ride into the foothills or to fetch a jar
of water, but to cross the irrevocable gulf of death. That gulf
may open at your feet at any hour and you may never return to
dry the tears of one you left weeping.*

KERISH awoke the next morning to the melancholy
sound of flutes and the wailing of horns. It was the
only sound permitted in all the city and a strict fast was
observed by everyone from the Emperor to the hungriest
urchin. In silence Kerish put on a thin robe of white and
gold, the mourning garments of the Godborn.

At noon, an escort of fifty soldiers of the Imperial
Guard, all cloaked in white, assembled in an inner courtyard of the Palace. The place was thronged with silent
courtiers, the women holding bitter herbs to their eyes to
make them seem red with weeping, the men huddled
together, exchanging knowing glances. Beneath the
enforced solemnity, the court was alive with rumour and
speculation.

The city was stunned. Always before the Emperors had
announced the impending deaths among the Godborn and
everyone had time to prepare. Rimoka had given out that
her daughter-in-law had died of a miscarriage but even
those who had not been present in the banqueting hall were
heard to doubt it.

Musicians entered the courtyard, playing the discordant
music of death, the destroyer of harmony. Behind them
walked Lord Izeldon leading a phyle of priests. Next came
a magnificent, golden palanquin hung with white. Inside
lay Gankali, dressed in her bridal clothes, the fine silk

97

strained over her fruitful belly. The litter was borne by the eldest of the male Godborn present: Jerenac, Im-lo-Torim and the Crown Prince.

Gankali's husband now appeared perfectly composed but his cheek bore the traces of a blow from Queen Rimoka. Impotent to punish the murderess, she had turned her fury on her son, railing at him for betraying his weakness before court and Ambassador.

Now she, too, appeared quite calm as she walked barefoot and white-robed behind the litter. Behind her came Kelinda, her pale face drawn with tiredness, leading her husband's three-year-old daughter; Kerish-lo-Taan, and the ladies, officials and pages of Gankali's household followed.

Forollkin mounted a white horse and led the escort through the Palace and out into the city. The wailing of horns warned the citizens of their presence and there was no one to watch the funeral procession pass by, for the Galkians were forbidden to look at the unveiled faces of the royal mourners.

It took two weary hours to pass through the city and the distance from the gates to the Valley of Silence was more than four miles. It was a long and exhausting walk. The bearers of the litter were forbidden to rest and, tired and bewildered, the little Princess Koligani began to sob. Rimoka turned round once to cuff her grandchild into silence but a mile from the city the sobs turned into screams and Koligani crouched down and refused to move. Kelinda did her best to soothe the child without actually speaking but Kerish slipped forward and lifted the girl in his arms. Ignoring the Queen's scowls of disapproval he carried the little Princess all the way, though his back and shoulders ached with her plump weight. He even allowed her to amuse herself by tugging at his hair and making him pull faces.

At last, in late afternoon, they reached the gateway of the Valley of Silence. Lord Izeldon motioned for the litter to be set down and the weary bearers gladly obeyed. The Crown Prince knelt and drew back the white curtains and lifted Gankali from the palanquin.

The escort and the Princess's household halted at the archway; only the Godborn entered the valley itself. The place was as beautiful as when Kerish had last seen it and his tiredness dropped away as they descended into the gulf of silence. The grass was soft and moist beneath his feet and the air was heavy with the scent of a million star-flowers.

The pale figures of the Godborn moved like sleep-walkers towards the heart of the valley. There, ugly amid the rich beauty of the iranda, the dark earth gaped. Gently the Crown Prince laid Gankali in her shallow grave and, at a touch from Kelinda, released her hand.

Silently the High Priest prayed for the dead and then he gathered an armful of star-flowers and cast them on her body. One by one the Godborn copied him until Gankali's form was lost beneath a mound of scented blossoms.

Laughing, the little Princess joined in this strange new game and covered her mother's face with petals. The Queen of Galkis was the last to honour the dead and there was no scorn in her face as she let the blossoms fall.

The funeral was over and the Godborn left the Valley of Silence without looking back. Beyond the archway horses were now waiting for the tired mourners to ride back to the city but they could not yet rest. The night must be spent in elaborate festivities. The whole city would rejoice at the passing of Gankali's soul into the realm of Zeldin but behind the smile that custom exacted from a royal mourner the Crown Prince's face was as blank and desolate as his mad cousin's.

For the next three days Kerish watched his apartments being stripped of furniture and ornaments and his jewels, furs and clothes packed into carrying chests. Everything had to appear as if he were permanently moving his whole household to Ephaan. Messengers had already been sent along the Royal Road to alert the nobles and officials who would have to entertain the Prince on his journey.

Forollkin was constantly busy organizing the details of their escort and baggage but Kerish soon discovered that there was nothing he could usefully do. To escape the turmoil in his quarters, Kerish frequently retreated to his own small garden and as he sat reading beside a fountain on the third morning, a flustered servant approached.

"Your Highness, the Ambassador of Oraz desires to speak to you."

Kerish's thoughts swirled in confusion and then settled. He remembered that today the Ambassador was to have his long-delayed audience with Queen Rimoka, indeed by now it must be over.

"Ask his Excellency to come to me here in the garden."

A few minutes later Khan O-grak was announced.

The Ambassador was alone. Kerish inclined his head slightly.

"I am honoured, my Lord Ambassador, though why you should . . ."

"I'll come to my purpose at once," said O-grak, and sat down beside the startled Prince on the edge of the fountain.

"I am sick of weaving words with the rest of your kin. Do you know why I was sent here?"

"To announce the new alliance of the Five Kingdoms and perhaps to raise the question of the Jenozan border?"

The Ambassador nodded. It was an old quarrel. Oraz and Jenoza were separated by the river Jenze but the river did not mark the boundary. The Galkian Empire extended twenty miles to the west of the Jenze and the Princes of Oraz had always claimed that twenty miles as their territory.

"The Prince, my nephew," began Khan O-grak, "has instructed me to demand that the territory beyond the Jenze be restored to Oraz."

"Demand is a strong word, my Lord!"

"And backed by strong swords. To be plain, if the land is not yielded, Oraz and her allies will declare war on your Empire."

Kerish trailed a hand through the clear waters of the fountain.

"My Lord, I am sure the Queen has already refused you. Why do you tell this to me?"

"Prince, you seem to store some wits behind those eyes of yours, and I hear your father, the Emperor, favours you. Go to him, then, persuade him of the justice of our cause . . . There's no need to flare at me," growled O-grak. "I offer no bribe but the thought of saving your country from a needless war."

"And if I were to do as you ask, what would your Prince demand next? The whole of Jenoza perhaps?" asked Kerish. "No, we cannot give up the land beyond the river, if only for the sake of those your Priests of Az would persecute and slaughter."

"Your people may pray to your pale young god as much as they like, though it is true that they would have to give up your Foremother and acknowledge the Lady of Blood as their only goddess."

"That they will never do!" declared Kerish.

"Then they will die," said O-grak calmly, "and think themselves blessed for it no doubt. So your answer is 'no'?"

Kerish nodded.

"Well, I am glad. I love defiance," announced O-grak, "and this will be a brave war. I will remember you for your courtesy, Prince Kerish-lo-Taan, when I burn your city of Ephaan. I will spare your life and I will take you home to be a prettier present for my wife even than your bracelet. My word on it, Prince: for your brothers the sword, but for you soft captivity."

"You are too kind, my Lord Ambassador!" said Kerish, his voice shaking with anger. "I will remember you also when the wrath of Zeldin is unleashed on Oraz."

The Ambassador laughed. "Keep to that faith, Prince, or despair may kill you before I can fasten an iron collar around your neck."

He rose and bowed mockingly and then stood tugging his fingers through his stiff, black beard.

"This is a fair garden. We have nothing like it in Oraz."

Before Kerish could think of a stinging answer, the Ambassador had gone.

Forollkin's face was very grave when he listened as Kerish repeated the gist of his conversation with O-grak.

"It would have been wiser to pretend to consider the demand," said Forollkin. "We need time to put the defences of Jenoza in good order."

"Rimoka has too much of the barbarian's own temper for that," answered Kerish. "Do you still wish you were going to Jenoza?"

"Yes," said Forollkin, and went back to planning their journey to Ephaan.

The next day Kerish was received by the Queen and the Crown Prince, given copious advice on the government of Ephaan and kissed coldly on the cheek. In the afternoon he took Forollkin with him to say goodbye to Kelinda. The young soldier had never been to the Princess's apartments before, and he was startled both by their almost drab simplicity and by the quantities of books and scrolls heaped in every available space. Kelinda rose hurriedly from a window seat and came forward to greet them.

"I am sorry if we have disturbed you in the middle of a poem," said Kerish.

"Oh no, I was just copying out a fable for Koligani and trying to draw pictures to go with it. Birds and beasts and flowers I can manage, but my people! Dry twigs have more life."

Kelinda realized that she was still clutching her dripping quill. She set it down, asked her guests to be seated and sent one of her ladies to fetch wine.

While they waited, Kerish asked the Princess about her step-daughter.

"She has begun to understand that her mother will never come back," answered Kelinda, "but sometimes she still screams or cries for her."

"Doubtless the Crown Prince is a comfort to her," said Forollkin stiffly.

"No. That is, he would be," stammered Kelinda, "but he is greatly upset by her crying. The Crown Prince likes to have happy faces surrounding him."

"Then he is born in the wrong age..." Kerish broke off as a servant entered with a flagon and two cups of rose crystal. Kelinda poured wine for her guests but did not join them. It was not the Seldian custom for ladies to eat or drink in company, and Kelinda only hardened herself to do so on state occasions.

"Your health, Princess," said Forollkin and there was a nervous pause as Kerish searched for the words to begin saying goodbye.

"I envy you living in Ephaan," Kelinda suddenly broke the silence. "From my journey here, I remember it as a beautiful city and you will always be within the sound of the sea. The Jorgan Isles will also be in your care, I suppose, though perhaps you do not intend to visit them, with the passage of the Sea of Az so dangerous."

"It will be one of our first tasks to remedy that," said Forollkin.

Kelinda smiled timidly at the young captain, whom she scarcely knew.

"You have sailed often?"

"Yes, ... well only on the state barges, but I expect it's much the same," said Forollkin airily.

"Say that to your ships' captains and they'll mutiny! Is throwing sticks the same as firing an arrow?"

Forollkin, who had never expected to be teased by the grave Princess of Seld, muttered into his wine-cup.

"Promise me, Lord Forollkin," said Kelinda abruptly, "not to be too brave, nor to let Kerish be either. The Brigands show no mercy!"

"Lady, I cannot make that promise for myself," answered Forollkin grimly, "but I will keep Kerish safe."

"You'll go grey-haired trying," protested Kerish.

Kelinda turned to him. "And you, brother in Zeldin, will you promise to write often? I shall miss a companion in my studies."

"No, I can't promise either... Kelinda, don't be upset," Kerish seized her thin ink-stained hand.

"I am not upset," said Kelinda. "I do not know your customs and if it is unfitting..."

"It's nothing like that. Kelinda, I cannot write because we will not be staying in Ephaan."

"Kerish!"

"Forollkin, it's all right," declared the Prince. "I know we can trust Kelinda."

Looking at her grave face and compassionate grey eyes, Forollkin could well believe it.

"Yes," he thought a little bitterly, "I can trust a stranger but not my own kin, not my mother..."

"Kelinda you must say nothing to anyone and when the

news comes you must pretend ignorance," insisted Kerish. "We are not leaving the city to govern Ephaan, but to seek the Saviour."

As neither of Kelinda's attendants understood High Galkian, Kerish was free to speak and he told her everything he knew about their quest.

She listened quietly, her hands knotted in her lap and said finally: "And you believe that this is Zeldin's will?"

"Yes," answered Kerish.

"I don't know," said Forollkin, "but it is the High Priest's and he's the nearest I'll get to Zeldin."

"I withdraw my request," murmured Kelinda. "You will need all your bravery. Kerish, you say it is possible that you might visit Seld?"

The Prince nodded.

"Then take this ring." Kelinda drew a plain circle of emerald from her finger. "If you meet my sister, the Queen, give this to her as a token, and she will welcome you."

"Have you any message for your sister?" asked Kerish.

"Yes, tell her that she was right, and that if I had my life again, I would never stir from the Temple of Trykis."

They left shortly afterwards and for the first time Kelinda's household heard their mistress weep.

In the cool of the evening Kerish wandered through the Emperor's garden. He hardly knew what impulse had brought him there. He had received no summons from his father and he ought to have stayed in the Palace. Forollkin would be angry but still Kerish lingered as the sun faded. There was no wind, and it was very still. The flowers, robbed of colour by the setting sun, looked pale and deformed. The trees seemed to lean threateningly towards him; the vines and creepers to reach out for his hands and throat.

Kerish remembered all the whispered stories he had heard about the Emperor's garden. Stories of men who had climbed the wall to see the wonders within or to pick a flower for their sweethearts, and who had never returned. Once he, himself, had found a yellowing skull among a clump of innocent blue flowers. A night bird cried and Kerish ran.

Desiring only to get out of the garden he fled down twisting paths and missed his way. In sudden panic he found himself running into a part of the garden he did not know. Unheeding, Kerish splashed across a green rivulet. The water was icy and soaked through his thin clothes in seconds. The garden was silent and still, as if it had drawn breath before some sudden, violent action. Kerish ran blindly on till, tumbling through a seemingly solid hedge, he fell face down on the grass. He lay quietly there till his heartbeat slowed and he began to be ashamed of his irrational terror.

Angry with himself, Kerish sat up and looked about. He was inside a circle formed by the high, thorn hedge through which he had crashed in his panic. In front of him was a strange building, like a pointed tent of embroidered cloth but all carved in white stone. The doorway was uncovered and from inside a voice said softly: "Kerish? Come inside, child."

The Prince entered a richly furnished, circular chamber, dominated by the object that lay in the centre of the room. Long and low, carved of purest alabaster in the form of a sleeping girl, it was a coffin for a Queen and beside it knelt the Emperor of Galkis.

Kerish stared at him and then, remembering his duty, prostrated himself.

Once more the Emperor gently drew his son to his feet.

"Welcome, Kerish, but you are trembling, your skin bleeds and your clothes are soaked. You have felt the terror that walks in the gardens of Galkis at evening?"

Kerish nodded and the Emperor smiled at him.

"Poor Kerish-lo-Taan, you are too sensitive to the horrors which lie beneath the mask of beauty. Forget them, or your life will torture you as mine tortures me."

"I can't help myself," whispered Kerish, "it is my birthright."

"Your birth curse!" said the Emperor. "The gracious gifts of Zeldin, of clear sight and foreknowledge, that sever us from humanity. Happy are the blind who cannot see the face of truth; happy are the deaf who cannot hear the promise of hope."

"Father," protested Kerish, "if you had been blind and deaf, you would never have seen my mother's face or heard her vows of love!"

"Or have grieved for her death," said the Emperor coldly.

"Will you have nothing then for fear of losing everything; take pleasure in nothing for fear of it turning to grief?" demanded Kerish. "How can you bear such emptiness? I would rather have grief than never know joy!"

"You speak justly," sighed the Emperor, "but you are young and brave. A man's courage is like the oil in a lamp, the brighter it is the more swiftly it burns away. It cannot be replenished and at last the lamp goes out and leaves you in the dark . . ."

"Father!" Forgetting all custom and precedent, Kerish flung his arms around the Emperor. "Father, however deep the darkness, you can share another's light. You need not be alone. There are many who would love you if you let them. The High Priest, the Princess Kelinda, your granddaughter . . ."

"But I do not love them," stated the Emperor.

Kerish let him go and stepped back a pace. "Nor anyone?"

The Emperor did not answer directly but knelt by the alabaster sarcophagus.

"Do you know who lies here?"

Kerish looked down at the alabaster face.

"Queen Taana?"

"Yes, your mother. She was sixteen when they brought her to the Palace," murmured Ka-Litraan. "The Brigands of Fangmere caught my Taana when they raided the windy plains of Erandachu. They sold her to a slave merchant of Mintaz who brought her to Ephaan. The Governor saw her and bought Taana as a gift for his Emperor. They had to throw her down before me. She would not prostrate herself even to the Emperor of Galkis. I could love her but I could not change her. She did not know the shape of fear or falsehood."

The Emperor slid his hands along the smooth alabaster.

"And she was beautiful, Kerish. Deep, grey eyes and hair as silver as the light of a falling star. She was white as the northern snows and here she lies, as fair as the first day I saw her, fair and cold. When the darkness closes round me I take her from her tomb and hold her in my arms. Do you wish to see her, Kerish?"

"No, no!"

The Emperor looked up. "Don't be afraid, Kerish. Perhaps you are right to think me mad, but I would never harm her son."

Kerish, his back against the marble wall, could frame no answer. The Emperor stared at him hungrily and then the expression in his eyes changed.

"Child, you're shivering and tired. Take off that wet robe and I will find you something warmer."

The Emperor crossed the small room and opening a chest drew out a mantle of thick black fur. He tossed it to Kerish who slipped off his sodden robe.

"Sit down," commanded the Emperor.

The Prince obeyed and the Emperor waited on him, pouring out a cup of wine.

"Drink this!" Kerish sipped obediently. "It is late and dark, too dark for us to cross the gardens now. Even I might lose faith on such a night."

"I must go back, your Majesty," murmured Kerish. "Forollkin will worry."

Drowsiness was clouding his mind and his father's face wavered in the dim light.

"Let him. For this once you will stay. I have given you a potion that brings peaceful sleep. Tonight we shall rest together, the three of us."

Too tired to protest further, Kerish lay down on a couch, huddled in the fur mantle, and the Emperor of Galkis watched over him.

Sunlight flooding through the open doorway woke Kerish. He lay on a hard couch in a strange room and his father sat beside him. Kerish remembered the events of the evening and sat up, instantly awake.

"The sun is gilding Galkis," said the Emperor, "you

must go."

Kerish slid off the couch and dressed in his now dry robe. Hesitantly, the Prince knelt.

"Father, give me your blessing."

The Emperor smoothed down a stray whisp of silver hair.

"You have it always, child of my heart, and this gift I give you."

The Lord of the Godborn placed his hands on Kerish's forehead.

"The cruel gift of seeing Truth through the mists of illusion. Be brave, Prince of the Godborn, braver than I have ever been."

Kerish felt as if courage, as a tangible thing, flowed into him from his father's hands.

"Come then." The Emperor led his son out of Queen Taana's tomb to a gate in the thorn hedge.

"Take the left-hand path as far as the grove of amber-leaved trees. Then cross the jasper bridge and you will be in the Maze of Eldiss. From there you know your way."

Kerish nodded but still lingered by his father's side.

"Go," said the Emperor, "Forollkin is angry and even the High Priest is failing to soothe him."

"Goodbye, my Lord."

Childlike, Kerish hugged his father. For a moment the Emperor held him close and kissed him on the forehead. Then he pushed him gently away and repeated: "Go."

Kerish walked slowly through the gate but ran towards the grove and all the way back to the Inner Palace. The Emperor of Galkis stared after him and then opened his arms to embrace the darkness of Taana's tomb.

Forollkin paced Kerish's empty apartments, slapping a riding whip against his leg.

"My dear Forollkin," began the High Priest for the third time, "I assure you your Prince is safe."

"I don't doubt your word," said Forollkin, unconvincingly, "but safe or not, why isn't he here? There were a thousand and one things to be done last night and I was left to struggle with them all!"

"Would you really have let him help if he had been

here?" murmured the High Priest but Forollkin swept on.

"To be gone all night and never a message to tell me where he is! When he does come back I'll flay him, I'll . . ."

"I think I'll run away again," said Kerish, who had been standing unnoticed in the doorway for more than a minute.

"Kerish, where in Zeldin's name have you been?" Forollkin shook his half-brother by the shoulders. "I've had the Imperial Guard out looking for you!"

"I have been with the Emperor," answered Kerish quietly.

Izeldon, who had been studying the Prince's pale face said: "Don't scold, Forollkin. The Emperor must be obeyed."

"Well, I suppose it was not your fault," muttered Forollkin ungraciously. "Your travelling clothes are laid out on your bed. Be quick, now, the escort is waiting."

When the Prince had gone, Izeldon said: "Be gentle with Kerish today. Parting is bitter and he has begun to understand his father's torment."

Forollkin made no answer. He was thinking of his own parting with his mother and the lying promises he had made to her.

"So all is ready," continued Izeldon. "Your efficiency is much to be praised, Forollkin, but there is one thing you must pay special attention to outside Galkis, and that is secrecy. Once beyond Ellerinonn it would normally be wiser to travel as ordinary Galkians, not Lords of the Godborn. I will speak no names, but more than one of the Godborn would look on the return of a Saviour as a threat to their own power. In addition to that, the older Kerish became, the more pressure would have been put on him to side with one party or the other in the coming struggle. Now he is standing aside from both, so both may try to prevent his ever returning to Galkis. Do you understand?"

"Yes," said Forollkin, "you don't have to speak the names. We will be wary in lands that acknowledge the power of the Godborn, though I fear Kerish will not take easily to travelling as a common man. For all he speaks of freedom he is used to the trappings of royalty."

"Yes, you will both find it hard," murmured Izeldon.

"I am ready. I have been very quick." Kerish re-entered the room. He wore the rich travelling dress of a Lord of the Godborn and his purple cloak was swathed round his head, covering all but his eyes.

"You have the Jewel of Zeldin?" asked the High Priest.

Kerish nodded. It hung beneath his tunic, cold against his skin.

"Wear it always, but think of it as a trust, not a possession. Forollkin, I have a gift for you too." The High Priest held out a slim dagger. "Take this. It will never fail you. It will kill swiftly and mercifully and it is the first weapon that I have ever blessed."

Forollkin bowed and murmured his thanks.

"There is much I could say," declared Izeldon, "but probably to little purpose. Do whatever the King of Ellerinonn asks of you and be loving brothers. Now, since your escort waits, I will ride to the city gates with you."

Led by Forollkin on his roan mare, the escort of the new Governor of Ephaan passed through the Golden City. Kerish-lo-Taan's litter was surrounded by marching soldiers and followed by fifty pack-ponies. At the outer gate Forollkin dismounted and Kerish's litter was set down. The High Priest spoke sombrely to them both.

"You have my blessing. In trouble and torment, in splendour and sorrow my love goes with you. May Zeldin the Gentle have mercy and Imarko the Wise guide you."

Forollkin saluted and returned to the head of the column. Kerish looked up at the High Priest and whispered:

"My Lord, I wish to thank you for the trust you have placed in me. Will we meet again?"

The High Priest stooped to embrace him. "Not while I live." He turned away.

Forollkin gave the signal and the Prince's litter was lifted. The escort marched through the gate and on to the Royal Road to Ephaan. Lying face down among the purple cushions of his litter, Kerish did not once look back at the High Priest or at the Golden City he might never see again.

Chapter 9

The Book of the Emperors: *Wisdom*

*The virtue of a journey rarely lies in its destination. What
man is so closed to thought that he will not be brought to wonder
whether it is he who moves, or the world?*

IN the blazing noonday sun Kerish-lo-Taan was leaning
over the rail of a ship staring down into the calm waters
of the Great Harbour at Ephaan. Within its sheltering
walls, the sea was the colour of pale amethysts and so clear
that Kerish could see the shape of every rock that jutted
through the white sand three fathoms below. The surface
of the water, ruffled by a slight breeze all morning, was
now smooth as glass, a glass that offered the Prince his
reflection.

How often he had longed for one forbidden glimpse of
his face. Kerish made out a dark, shapeless figure. His
head, and half his face, were swathed, as custom demanded, in purple cloth, but Kerish could see a band of
white where his skin was uncovered, and the dark hollows
that were his eyes... A stone, dropped from above, shattered the glassy surface and broke the Prince's reflection
into a thousand ripples.

Kerish turned angrily to face a smiling Forollkin.

"Do you remember how the priests ceremonially beat
you once for staring into a pool? Well, don't forget the law.
It was made for more than the checking of vanity, or so the
priests tell us."

"I was watching a shoal of silvery-green fish," said
Kerish quickly.

"Indeed? I saw none." Forollkin was sceptical.

"They have just swum under the ship," insisted the
Prince.

111

Forollkin was tempted to ask what kind they were, but he knew he could never catch his brother out on such details. Kerish was perfectly capable of inventing a dozen different kinds of fish and describing them minutely. Instead, he merely delivered his news:

"We are ready to sail."

Forollkin's efficiency had made the long journey from Galkis to Ephaan swift and trouble-free. After riding hard every day, at night they had either camped by the Royal Road or been obsequiously received into the homes of nobles and officials. The people might curse their ineffectual rulers in distant Galkis but the presence of an actual Prince of the Godborn still drew them, and spurred them to reverence.

For the first time in his life, Kerish had been treated, not as the youngest son, the least important, but as a mighty Prince. Everything that he admired in the house of his hosts was instantly offered to him. Had he been of age, it would have been not just jewels and ornaments but their wives and daughters too, since to bear a child to one of the Godborn was considered a high honour.

He was not too young, however, for people to flock to the roadside and dart forward to kiss the hem of his cloak. Craftsmen begged Kerish to touch their hands or the tools of their trade and farmers beseeched him to tread on their soil and bless their animals. Intoxicated by their faith, Kerish-lo-Taan had graciously done all they asked. Disgusted, Forollkin had seen his brother begin to accept such worship as his due. To the young captain, the people's faith was a forlorn and pitiable thing. Nothing would persuade him that Kerish was divine.

So at last they had come to Ephaan, the great copper-walled city by the shores of the purple sea. After a ceremonial welcome the puzzled Governor had humbly asked for some explanation of his Emperor's strange orders. Kerish had told him that he was on a secret mission of great importance and that he required a ship to cross the Sea of Az. It was to be announced that the new Governor was visiting the Jorgan Isles. The anxious Governor protested

112

against the dangers of such a journey since the Jorgan Islands now paid tribute to the ships of Fangmere that hid in their harbours, waiting to attack the traffic in the sea lanes.

Kerish-lo-Taan had rebuked the Governor for his lack of faith in Zeldin's power to protect his children but the old man had been politely obdurate and in the end the Prince had been forced to accept an escort of three triremes. Kerish and Forollkin themselves were to travel in the swiftest and most beautiful ship in the Galkian fleet, the *Zeloka*.

On their fifth morning in Ephaan, they had visited the ship. Kerish had admired the great figurehead carved and gilded like a zeloka with wings outspread, and approved his small but sumptuously furnished cabin. He had also sent aboard a ridiculous quantity of luggage and refused to give the captain any information about the destination of their voyage.

Forollkin had quietly had some of the luggage offloaded and had taken Captain Engis aside. Over a cup of iced wine he had explained the probable length of their journey to the worried captain so that he could arrange the necessary provisions. Two days later there had been a formal banquet to welcome Kerish as Governor and the next morning they had boarded the *Zeloka* again.

"We're ready to sail," repeated Forollkin. Half an hour later they stood together on deck as the *Zeloka* sailed away from the crowded wharf, past the slave market where Kerish's mother had once been sold.

"I would have forbidden it," he said abruptly.

Forollkin understood him. "It is against our ancient custom, but at least slaves are better treated here than in any other land."

"Yes. We burden them with gratitude to complete their slavery."

The *Zeloka* passed a dozen merchant ships of Forgin, two royal galleys of Seld, a quinquereme of Mintaz and five longships of Dard, to reach the entrance to the Great Harbour. As they came out into the open sea the ship plunged and the wind assaulted the purple and golden sails.

Forollkin stared back at Ephaan till all he could see was the occasional flash of sunlight on the copper walls. Beside him Kerish unwound his purple headcloth and veil and tossed them into the wind.

"Kerish!"

"I am sick of being veiled and while we're at sea I refuse to hide my face."

"It is the law," protested Forollkin.

"It is now, but Mikeld-lo-Taan never hid himself from his people and nor will I," declared Kerish. "Besides, we're beyond the reach of the law now."

"That's not what the priests say. Zeldin is Lord of all Zindar," said Forollkin stiffly.

"But Zindar is full of gods and goddesses too."

"Kerish! That's sacrilege. Someone might hear."

The Prince laughed. "Don't sound so shocked, brother. I think the High Priest would say that Zeldin is the god of Zindar only if your prayers make him so. Do you pray to him?"

"Yes. No. You shouldn't ask."

Kerish softened. "I'm sorry, you're right. I shouldn't ask, but sometimes I think you treat Zeldin as a soldier would the General of his army. You accept his orders without question through his officers, but you don't ever want to meet the General himself."

"If every soldier chased after orders direct from the General, no army could march," said Forollkin briskly, "and I don't have the time to fool with such thoughts."

He went below to check their baggage for the third time.

To the captain's despair, Kerish spent the rest of the day exploring the *Zeloka,* disrupting work wherever he went. Each time he passed, the sailors prostrated themselves and avoided looking at his face. In the small space of a busy ship it was difficult to observe these courtesies. Sometimes he stopped to talk to members of the crew who stared fixedly at the deck and stuttered timidly.

Having found out everything about the workings of the ship he settled on the poop-deck and harrassed the captain further by constantly despatching sailors to fetch him books, glasses of wine, cloaks and scarves. In the late afternoon a strong tail wind blew up, sweeping them along their route and making the *Zeloka* rise and dip in the swell. This did nothing to mar Kerish's enjoyment but Forollkin was humiliatingly sick.

He lay in his cabin, vomiting every few minutes while his world heaved as if trying to give birth to a monster. After an excellent supper Kerish came down to Forollkin's cabin, solicitously carrying a bowl of soup. Forollkin smelt it and was sick again. Kerish chattered brightly about the pleasures of shipboard life until his half-brother hissed at him to go away. Forollkin consoled himself through the long rough night with visions of strangling Kerish, and fell asleep just before dawn.

The Prince was up early and still feverishly active. He paced round and round the deck staring at drifts of seaweed, green and gold against the purple sea, leaping shoals of coppery fish and skeins of sea-birds flying eastward. Near mid-morning Forollkin staggered on to deck. Kerish steadied him.

"I'm glad to see you looking less green. The seaweed was more companionable than you yesterday."

"It is hard to be entertaining when you're spewing like a geyser," retorted Forollkin.

Kerish opened his mouth to say that he had found that very entertaining, but thought better of it.

"Never mind, you're recovering, let's take a cup of wine with the captain."

Before Forollkin could say that his stomach felt too frail to take a cup of anything Kerish was half-way across the poop-deck.

The captain of the *Zeloka* and half his crew, including the man at the wheel, knelt while Kerish arranged himself comfortably on a couch beneath a purple awning. He then gave them permission to rise.

"Captain Engis, you will drink some wine with us."

"Your Highness I am deeply honoured," answered Engis with a melancholy smile, "but at this moment I have much to do. With so strong a tail wind we are getting too far ahead of our triremes and . . ."

"Captain Engis, I am not interested in our triremes."

Kerish's tone was very sweet but the captain winced. "As you said, you are deeply honoured."

The Prince signalled for the wine to be brought. Engis stifled several sacrilegious thoughts and bowed submissively.

Stools were brought for Forollkin and the captain and the hot, spiced wine was served.

"To the most beautiful ship in the Sea of Az!" proclaimed Kerish.

"And the swiftest too, your Highness." Engis gulped down his wine. "I remember her Highness, the Princess of Seld, being gracious enough to say that she sped over the waves like a real bird in flight."

"Have you had many such royal passengers?" asked Forollkin.

"Yes indeed, my Lord, and the first on the *Zeloka*'s maiden voyage, the Princess of Chiraz, that is Queen now. I was second mate then and I remember her well, a handsome lady, if you'll forgive my saying it, and so eager to get to Galkis that she promised rewards to every member of the crew if we could cut two days off the crossing. I still have the Chirazian gold coin she gave me. I never had the heart to spend it. I had it pierced for an amulet instead. Not, of course, that the servants of Zeldin need such things," added Engis hastily.

The Prince had not noticed his indiscretion. He was trying to imagine his step-mother as a young girl anxious for love.

"Father," he thought, "why were you so cruel to those you couldn't love?"

"What is that land over there? That black hump on the horizon?" asked Forollkin.

"That's the Isle of Az, my Lord. This is the closest we'll sail to it, for it's an evil place, by all I've ever heard."

"It is there that the Dark Goddess has her temple," murmured Kerish.

"Yes, your Highness," said Engis, "the temple of Idaala, Lady of Blood, and with blood they worship her. They say there is a living goddess in the temple. Each year the priests of Az choose a consort for her and each year she

116

murders him."

"And it is her worshippers who snatch at our Empire!"

"Zeldin preserve us all," said Engis grimly.

"What's the island to the west there?" asked Forollkin, trying to shake off the darkness that spread from Az.

"Ah, that's one of the seven islets, each with a spring of fresh water and a good deep anchorage," said Engis. "They're a great blessing to sailors and men call them the Footsteps of God."

"I remember," murmured Kerish, "when Zeldin wanted to cross the sea from Galkis to Ellerinonn he became tall as the stars. He crossed the sea in seven great strides and in the seven places where he wished to set down a foot, islands sprang up."

"Ay, that's the tale, your Highness. A true one no doubt," said Engis quickly, recalling that the Prince claimed descent from that same god.

"Do the Brigands of Fangmere use the Footsteps?" asked Forollkin.

Engis nodded. "Yes my Lord, though even ten years ago they would not have dared. Now their ships haunt the whole sea. No passage is safe, and even close to the Galkian coast you'll find them hovering to snatch an unescorted merchant vessel or a careless pleasure craft."

"What are their ships like?" asked Kerish.

"Narrow, nearly as swift as the *Zeloka,* but strong enough to ram almost anything. They hunt in pairs and they'll strip a vessel of its cargo, and burn it, kill the old and the weak and take the rest for slaves, all in an hour. It's said that if they fail to capture a ship they must give Idaala her blood sacrifice from among their own men, and that spurs them on."

"The world is full of horrors," murmured Kerish.

"Well I've shuddered enough," announced Forollkin. "Let's talk of something more pleasant."

"Yes." Kerish sat up straight. "Captain, I have often heard praises of the chants that Galkian sailors sing. Let us hear some."

"Kerish, the captain and his crew have to sail this ship," said Forollkin reasonably. "They cannot spend all day

117

entertaining you."

Kerish did not look at him.

"Lord Forollkin, what I choose to command is none of your concern. You will give the order, captain."

"Yes, your Highness." Engis got up to call together the best singers but Forollkin suddenly pushed past him and went below to his cabin. Kerish sat for an hour listening to the chants, smiling nervously.

If Engis noticed a coolness between the brothers in the succeeding week, he was careful not to show it. Kerish's fascination with the ship rapidly turned to boredom and he spent hours of every day pacing restlessly round the deck. When the southernmost of the Jorgan Isles was sighted the Prince leaned eagerly over the rail to watch the land take shape. When they were close enough to see the villages on the rocky slopes Captain Engis approached him.

"Your Highness, if we *were* sailing to Jorg, there lies our way." He pointed to a narrow channel between two islands. "Jorg itself is on the central isle and difficult to reach. The channel gets narrower further on and you need good charts or a native pilot not to founder on the rocks."

"Presumably the Brigands of Fangmere have both," said Kerish bitterly.

"Ay, your Highness, may the wind shred their sails!" muttered Engis. "They know every channel and current and rock. They sail in and out of these islands like children dodging behind trees in a game of Seek, and Zeldin himself couldn't catch them, if you'll forgive the expression."

Kerish was hardly listening. "I shall write to the Governor at Jorg informing him that I am inspecting the outer isles with six ships of war and that I expect to find everything put in order for my visit."

Engis grinned. "The shock will whiten his beard, your Highness. You wish to send one trireme, then, with the letter?"

"No, all three. I have no need of soldiers or ships of war; my mission lies under Zeldin's protection."

"But your Highness, only the coast of Ellerinonn itself is safe and we won't reach that for some days." Engis was clearly dismayed. "These islands are infested with Brigand ships..."

"Captain, I have made up my mind," snapped the Prince. "Give the order."

Kerish went to his cabin to write the letter and Engis sought out Forollkin. He repeated the warnings about the dangers of travelling unescorted off the Jorgan Isles, but Forollkin only said bitterly: "If his Highness has made up his mind there is nothing I can do. It is not my responsibility."

An hour later a long boat carried the Prince's letter to the captain of the leading trireme and the three warships turned north and entered the narrow channel. With a fair wind still behind her the *Zeloka* skimmed across the purple waves towards Ellerinonn.

In the noonday heat Kerish lay on his couch beneath the awning. Forollkin was somewhere below. A gentle breeze turned the pages of his book and the ship was at its quietest. Suddenly, through the drowsy calm, came a screech like a sea-bird's. Kerish swung himself off the couch. His book fell to the deck. He shaded his eyes against the sun and looked round. The cry sounded again and Kerish realized that it came from the lookout high in the crow's nest. A second later he understood what the man was saying.

"Fangmere! A Brigand ship!"

A hatch was thrown open. Engis, Forollkin and several crewmen clattered on to the deck. The captain shouted up to his lookout, listened for a moment and then strode to the rail with Forollkin at his heels. He stared northward for a minute and then turned, cursing, to bellow orders at his crew. To Forollkin the thing that menaced them was only a blurred shape against the horizon but to Kerish's long-sighted eyes it was horribly clear.

A ship of war, its treble bank of oars scything the waters, was coming towards them with great force and speed. A ship the colour of blood with the mark of the Dark Goddess emblazoned on its sail. Captain Engis had a few precious minutes to decide whether to keep on course and try to outrun the Brigand vessel or to waste time in turning, and head for the comparative safety of the nearest

Jorgan village.

Engis spoke first to Forollkin: "On the closest island there's a village with a good harbour. It's an easy place to defend and I think the people will be loyal to us. If we can reach it."

At a nod from Forollkin, Engis gave the order to turn the ship. To Kerish and Forollkin the process seemed hideously slow as they hung over the rail watching the Brigand ship racing towards them. Soon they could make out the high prow, bound with iron, that would be used to ram the *Zeloka* when they were close enough.

At last the *Zeloka* was facing the islands but she no longer had the wind behind her to give her speed. Half the crew rushed to man the oars. Others were adjusting the great sail and three men heated a cauldron of pitch for fire-arrows. With noise and confusion all around them the Prince and his brother stood in a haven of helpless calm. The *Zeloka* was rounding the headland of the nearest isle when the lookout gave another cry of horror.

Minutes later the captain and crew saw what he had seen. A second Brigand ship had been hiding in the shelter of the bay. Now the *Zeloka* was caught between the two vessels.

"Lord Forollkin!" Grim-faced, Engis strode up to them. "They will try to board us. Fetch your sword and defend the hatchway. Your Highness, get below and lock your cabin door. If they break in, tell them who you are and they might ransom you."

He left them, to see to the placing of archers. Everywhere men were arming and taking up their stations for battle.

"Give me a sword!" Kerish called out but they ignored him.

The Prince pushed his way to the other side of the ship. In a few minutes the second Brigand vessel would be close enough to fasten on to the *Zeloka* with grappling hooks. Kerish could see the men of Fangmere crowding round the prow, iron hooks and chains in their left hands, swords or axes in their right. They were tall, white-skinned and white-haired, with eyes filled with the lust of battle for the glory of Idaala. An arrow whined through the air and thudded into the rail by Kerish's hand. He stared at it stupidly.

"Kerish, for Zeldin's sake, get below!"

It was Forollkin shouting at him, but, still staring at the oncoming ship, the Prince shook his head. The gap between the ships was closing fast: fifty yards, thirty, twenty, ten . . . grappling hooks flew through the air. The ships were locked together. A rain of fire-arrows came from the poop-deck and caught the sails of the Brigand vessel. The first of the Men of Fangmere leapt shrieking on to the deck, his white hair streaming behind him. An arrow pierced his throat and he fell, but others followed, swinging swords and axes and yelling the praises of Idaala.

Forollkin raced across the deck to his half-brother.

"Kerish! Are you mad? Get out of the way or they'll kill you."

"Give me a sword!" shouted Kerish over the rising din of battle.

"You've never handled a sword in your life. It would be slashed out of your hand at the first stroke. Get below!"

"No. I am a Prince of the Godborn and I won't run away."

In a few seconds the Men of Fangmere would reach the upper deck. Forollkin seized Kerish and pulled him towards the hatch. "If you were the Emperor himself it wouldn't stop them splitting your skull. You're no use in battle, so don't hinder those who are trying to protect you!"

Kerish attempted to twist out of his brother's grasp.

"Oh Zeldin curse you!" Forollkin grabbed hold of Kerish's long hair and pulled him through the hatchway. Kerish cried out in pain but he took no notice. Forollkin dragged his half-brother down a passage, opened the door of his cabin and flung him in.

"Now stay there! Come on deck and I swear I'll cut your throat myself. It will be a cleaner death than the Men of Fangmere would give you. Lock the door when I go out. Do you understand?"

Kerish held his hands to his aching head and whispered: "Yes."

Forollkin slammed the door.

"You!" One of his own men was hurrying down the passage with an armful of arrows. "I'll take those. You guard the Prince's cabin."

"Yes my Lord."

The soldier stood with his back against the door, his sword in his hand. Forollkin raced up on deck to find it covered with fighting men. He slammed down the hatch and stood on it, prepared to defend his half-brother to the death. A tall Brigand lunged at him with an axe. Forollkin ducked and the axe struck the rail behind him. In the second before the Brigand could pull it back Forollkin had thrust his sword in the man's stomach. His body slumped at Forollkin's feet.

The vessel they had sighted first would soon be close enough to disgorge a boarding party. Then, desperately outnumbered, there would be no hope. Forollkin shut out all other thoughts and concentrated on killing. Careless of his own defence, he received a slash across the thigh, but cut off the swordsman's hand. All around him men were isolated on islands of battle, fighting for their lives. Forollkin no longer thought about any of them, even Kerish. He was alone with death.

Three Brigands came towards him, one with an axe, two with swords. Forollkin drew his dagger, leaned back against the rail, and waited. Within seconds a double attack came. With a numbing blow his sword was knocked from his hand. Forollkin lurched forward and plunged his dagger into the chest of one of his opponents. The man died, but the second Brigand leapt on Forollkin trying to pin back his arms for the third to thrust him through.

It was then that Forollkin heard, above the clash of swords and the moans of the dying, horns urgently blowing. After a few seconds, the man he was struggling with wrenched himself away. Weak with loss of blood, Forollkin slumped to the deck, waiting for death, but no sword fell.

Lying huddled on his bed Kerish listened to the sounds of the bloody fight on the deck above; the clanging of swords, the thud of axes, the hiss of arrows, the war cries of the Brigands and the screams of their victims. Kerish pressed his hands over his ears and shut his eyes to banish the sight of a wounded man hurtling past his window into the sea below. Sick with terror and helplessness, Kerish tried to pray but his lips would not form the words. His prayer was a long cry of agony, launched into emptiness and there was no answering calm, only mounting fear.

"Forollkin," he whispered, "Oh Forollkin!"

Then he, too, heard the horns harshly blowing.

It was the signal for retreat and stumbling over the bodies of the dead the Men of Fangmere crowded back on to their ship, unhooking the grappling irons as they went. The first vessel had already swung round and was rowing swiftly away. Forollkin got up and staggered to where Engis stood at the rail. A few arrows still thudded into the deck, but the Brigands were in full retreat.

"Why?" Forollkin demanded. "Why?"

Engis ordered one of his uninjured crewmen to climb the masthead and they soon had their answer.

"Our triremes, Sir, our triremes!" He clambered down again. "All three, Sir, my Lord, sailing fast towards us."

"Zeldin and Imarko be praised!" whispered the captain.

All over the ship men were crouching to give thanks to the Gentle God. The first ship of Fangmere was already well away but the second was pursued, rammed and sunk. Soon Engis and Forollkin were welcoming the captain of the third trireme aboard.

"What made you come back?" asked Forollkin at once.

"We met a fishing craft in the narrowest part of the channel," answered the captain. "I'd seen no others all morning and I thought that strange, so we hailed the man and he told us that two ships of Fangmere had been lurking in the outer isles and had sailed off westward an hour before. I was afraid you might meet them, my Lord, so I gave the order to turn back."

"The Prince will reward you," promised Forollkin.

"I've many wounded and some dead," said Engis firmly. "I'll need the help of some of your crew, captain."

They began a tour of the deck to count the dead and

comfort the wounded, but weak with his own loss of blood Forollkin suddenly swayed and leaned against a rail.

"That's a bad slash," muttered Engis. "I'll take you below, my Lord."

The wound was deep enough to have partly severed a muscle and the leg was beginning to stiffen. Engis himself cleansed the slash.

"Let the pain come out through your lips, my Lord," said the captain as he probed the wound. "I'll think none the worse of you."

The door opened and Kerish came slowly into the cabin.

"They told me you were wounded," he said.

"His Lordship has taken a bad slash," Engis answered for him, "but it's nothing that won't mend."

"I will tend it then," said Kerish. "That's one skill I have learned."

"Your Highness, are you injured too? You look . . ."

"No. Please go back to your men. I know you must want to be with them."

Engis handed a damp cloth to the Prince and he finished bathing the wound, and then carefully bandaged the leg.

Forollkin noticed black bruises on his brother's wrists where he had seized them so roughly.

"I'm sorry that I hurt you," he said stiffly, "but I had no choice. You would have thrown your life away."

"But I only wanted to . . ."

"I've heard too much of what you want since we came aboard this ship!" exclaimed Forollkin. "I can't stop you in public, but by Zeldin, you deserve thrashing as a spoilt child, snatching everything that takes your fancy, with no thought for others . . . Try to act like a true Prince and don't get in the way of those whose job it is to protect you!"

"But I can't bear to be a burden. I want to protect myself! Teach me to handle a sword."

"You know it's forbidden. You'd never have been allowed to use a whip if the laws were strictly kept. Fighting is my task," declared Forollkin, lying back on the bed. "Yours is to persuade these sorcerers to give up their keys, nothing more."

"No," cried Kerish angrily, "I will not be helpless. If you won't teach me to protect myself, I'll find someone who will."

"That's what every child cries when its toys are taken away," said Forollkin brutally. "Now go on deck and reward your loyal soldiers."

For the rest of the voyage Forollkin was forced to keep to his cabin and Kerish was notably subdued. Engis seemed to have guessed something of what he must be feeling and spoke gently to him on the morning they sighted Ellerinonn.

"We can send back our escort, your Highness, we are safe now. No ship of Fangmere dares come as close as this to the shores of Ellerinonn."

The *Zeloka* anchored in a sheltered harbour, beneath a cliff that hid the Enchanter King's city from view. There were no buildings visible from the harbour at all, only a wide stair cut in the rock. There were no other ships moored and no people, but baskets of fruit and flowers were standing on the quay. On deck twelve men in burnished mail waited to escort the Prince to the Enchanter's palace.

Forollkin's leg was not healing well and he had no choice but to let Kerish go alone. He lectured his half-brother on how to behave to the King.

"Remember, he owes no allegiance to the Emperor, so don't try to command him. I just hope he does know something about this key. After all, he can't really be immortal. I suppose the power must have been handed down from generation to generation."

"That's not what the High Priest said."

"Oh well, I expect it was just his manner of talking," muttered Forollkin uncomfortably. "Your fillet's crooked again."

Kerish leaned submissively over the bed for Forollkin to straighten it.

The young captain surveyed his half-brother's glittering robe, jewelled sandals and great collar of gold and irivanee, shaped like a zeloka in flight, and nodded approvingly.

Kerish-lo-Taan went up on deck to wait for the return of the herald he had sent to King Elmandis. When he came he was alone and the expression on the man's face told Engis that something was wrong. The herald knelt at the Prince's feet and stuttered:

"Highness, I delivered your message to the King by the hand of his chamberlain, but he sends back this answer . . ."

"Go on," said Kerish coldly.

The man looked down at the deck. "Highness, the King says that he receives no embassies from any country, nor any visitors. Only those in need of healing may approach the Enchanter King. Highness, he will not see you."

There was a long silence and even the men of the escort stared at their Prince. Then Kerish said quietly: "Thank you for undertaking the errand. Captain, dismiss your men."

Returning to his cabin Kerish stood for a moment with closed eyes, his hands clutching the Jewel of Zeldin. Then he stripped off his collar and fillet and glittering tunic and kicked away his sandals. In his plain white under-robe he returned to the deck and, ignoring the whispers of the crew, spoke to the startled captain: "I shall go ashore now. I will try to be back by nightfall but do not take alarm, or allow Lord Forollkin to do so."

Engis smiled at his Prince for the first time.

"I will not, your Highness, but at least let me come with you. It's more than a mile to the city."

"No, but I thank you, captain. If I lose my way I have only to ask."

"And ask you will," Kerish told himself through gritted teeth as he reached the top of the cliff.

The city was still not in sight, only a seemingly endless orchard. It was a landscape of lush grass, shadowed by stately trees, laden with ripe fruit. The sounds of distant music and hushed laughter reached Kerish as he followed the single marble-paved path. He stopped several times to stare at marvellous statues of men and beasts that stood under the trees and he glimpsed a few of the inhabitants of

Ellerinonn, but they took little notice of him. They were tall, copper-skinned and fair-haired. Both men and women were dressed in long, white cloths that curved round the body and fell in graceful folds from shoulder to ankle with bright embroidery about the hem. They moved slowly and reflectively and smiled at him but did not speak.

Half an hour's quiet walk brought Kerish to the edge of Tir-Rinnon but it was not the magnificent, walled citadel that he had imagined. A modest, pillared mansion of white stone was surrounded by small, elegant houses set in spacious gardens. Here and there were pools and fountains and paved squares where people seemed to congregate, but there was no city gate or guard.

Kerish walked unchallenged into the heart of Tir-Rinnon until an old man seemed to take pity on him and spoke in fluent Zindaric: "Stranger, whom do you seek?"

"The Enchanter King," replied Kerish. "I would be grateful if you could tell me where to find him."

"Elmandis is in the Place of Fountains." He pointed out the way. "But you must know him when you find him."

Kerish thanked the man and followed the path he had indicated through an avenue of pleached trees. He kept his right hand clenched around the Jewel of Zeldin and tried to envisage the Enchanter King.

Within a circle of glossy trees hung with scented blossoms, five fountains played, their sparkling waters leaping from the maws of silver fishes. On the grass beside the fountains, and on marble benches, a group of men and women were sitting. Some were in grave conversation, some reading and others listening to the music of a lyre.

As they noticed the stranger, music and conversation faltered and they turned calm faces towards him. Abashed, Kerish glanced quickly at all of them. There were several old men but none of them had the look of a King, and no one wore any obvious token of leadership. He was about to swallow his pride and ask for guidance when he noticed a man sitting apart in the shadows.

He seemed neither very old nor very young. Like all the other men he was tall and copper-skinned with hair so fair it was almost white. He was simply dressed, yet Kerish sensed that he was set apart by more than distance. Alone of all the people he had seen in Ellerinonn this man's face lacked serenity. Ignoring the others, Kerish-lo-Taan walked across the Place of Fountains and knelt at the man's feet.

"Great King, wise Elmandis, I beg your help and healing for myself and for another."

King Elmandis looked for a long time into Kerish's face and then said softly: "It is our law that the supplicant must be received and the sick healed. Who is this other?"

"Lord King, it is my brother. He is wounded in the leg and it is painful and slow to heal."

"Slow, yes, but that is Time's way; can I outrun him?"

"Yes, for I think you are Time's master," answered Kerish, and saw a strange expression pass across Elmandis' face that seemed to disturb all those sitting close to him.

"You are right. Time crouches at my heel like a whipped dog and loves me as little. Tell me, why should I heal your brother?" asked Elmandis coldly. "The world is full of suffering, why should his be eased?"

Kerish thought for a moment and then said carefully: "Because it hurts him so much to be idle, he cannot be at ease with his thoughts, only with his actions; because he fears for me when I am without his protection; and because without his strength a quest that might save Golden Galkis will fail."

"Ah." For a moment the King was silent. He placed the tips of his fingers on Kerish's forehead and then murmured, "So you have come at last. I feared that was your errand, Prince Kerish-lo-Taan. Oh yes, I know you, the face of the Godborn is unmistakable. It is fortunate for you that you came as a supplicant. You have trapped me in my own law or I would give you a death that would make the torturers of Fangmere retch."

Only Kerish heard his words but the men and women close by sensed the hatred in his voice and looked at Elmandis as if he and not Kerish were the stranger.

"Lord King," whispered Kerish, "I don't understand."

"Child," said Elmandis, "you bring me my death, and the end of Ellerinonn."

The King rose to his feet and spoke more calmly: "Friends, on the ship that anchors in our harbour there are wounded men. If you are moved to pity go and give them what healing you can, but bring the Prince's brother to Tir-Rinnon."

A dozen men and women got up and walked towards the harbour.

"You knew about our encounter with the Men of Fangmere?" asked Kerish.

"There is little that takes place in the Sea of Az that I do not know of," answered Elmandis calmly. "But you spoke of healing for yourself. Walk with me and we will talk. You need not look so wary, Prince; hate you or not, I have promised to help you."

The King of Ellerinonn and the Prince of Galkis walked back together down the avenue and Kerish caught at the lowest branches and traced the shape of the large amber leaves. Elmandis did not hurry him and gradually the Prince began to talk.

"The High Priest promised that Zeldin and Imarko would protect us and I believed him. I scorned soldiers and ships of war. I sent the triremes away. I thought it was a test of my faith, but because I believed in Zeldin's protection Forollkin is wounded and men have died."

"You are unscathed, Prince," said Elmandis coolly. "The mistakes of those who are protected are often paid for in the blood of those they love. It is a hard thing to bear and rightly so. However, I think that you have mistaken pride for faith, as so many do."

"I did not mean to be proud."

Elmandis almost smiled. "Don't glower at me like a storm cloud, Prince; I won't run for shelter. Pride does not require an act of will, though humility does. You have been rash to think that Zeldin must work miracles for your sake. When the Brigands of Fangmere attacked your ship, what did you expect? A hand to plunge down from the sky and hurl your enemies beyond the furthest star? One man in a fishing boat was enough to save you.

"Zindar is governed by natural laws: the rocks, the plants, the seas, the animals, the humans of our world, interlock and are one. If Zeldin, who is beyond this world, uses his power to destroy a single man or beast or rock or flower, it will in time affect the history of all men and all things. Therefore he uses one link in the chain of life to protect another, so do not always look for wonders and do not always crave the help of Zeldin. Your captain may believe in his god, but he does not leave Zeldin to sail his ship. The hero does not refuse to lift his sword against the monster because he knows his god is the enemy of evil. Temper your faith with judgement."

Kerish snapped off a handful of twigs. "The High Priest told me to listen to your counsel and I will."

"However unwillingly?"

Now Kerish smiled. "Yes, Lord King, however unwillingly. Sir, you speak of Zeldin as one who knows his mysteries and loves him dearly."

"Knows him, yes, but I will not love him," said Elmandis with quiet vehemence. "If we are truly free to reject his love then I mean to do so. I have taught my people to live without a god and to glory in their humanity. No power of Zeldin could now break down the defences of Ellerinonn and compel my people to worship, but he is cunning and wounds me with his trust."

"Lord King, I have come to ask your help for Galkis, not to harm Ellerinonn."

"Can you walk through a field, Prince, without destroying some form of life?" asked Elmandis. "No. You, Kerish-lo-Taan, will destroy everything in your path. But come, your brother has already been brought to the Chamber of Healing. We will not leave him in pain any longer."

Forollkin lay on a couch staring up at a painted ceiling. He refused to be soothed by the gentle colours of the room or the soft cushions beneath his head and plucked restively at the garland a smiling child had hung about his neck.

"I am sorry if peaceful Tir-Rinnon is not to a soldier's liking," said a soft voice.

Forollkin jumped. Elmandis and Kerish had come in quietly through a curtained archway.

"Kerish! Your clothes, your jewels, what have you..."

"Your Majesty," Kerish broke in quickly, "may I present my half-brother, the Lord Forollkin?"

Startled, Forollkin looked for the first time at the tall man with eyes the colour of a restless sea or the wind-bowed grasses of the northern plains.

He tried to get up and bow but Elmandis pushed him back with strong hands.

"Lie still. Your brother is concerned about your wound and has asked me to heal you."

"Your Majesty is generous but truly there is no need. I've no wish to trouble you, and the wound..."

"You need not be afraid," said Elmandis dryly, "I am no petty swamp sorcerer conjuring with serpents, rotting leaves and the payments of the credulous. But perhaps you do not believe that any man has power enough to heal instantly?"

"No. I mean I don't know, your Majesty."

"Well you shall learn. Let me see the wound."

He swiftly undid the bandage as Kerish looked on anxiously. The wound was crusted with blood where Forollkin's restless movements had re-opened it. Elmandis touched the place very lightly and closed his eyes for a moment.

"There is no poison there," he said. "The hands of a Healer have already soothed the wound."

"Kerish tended it for me," murmured Forollkin.

Elmandis seized the Prince's hands and studied them.

"Yes, a Healer's hands. I cannot hate you as I should. Kerish, fetch me the two chalices standing on the table there."

Kerish brought them and Elmandis took first a chalice of pale shining cirge patterned with the dark Flowers of Sleep. He held it to Forollkin's lips.

"Drink!"

Reluctantly Forollkin took a sip. "What is it?" he whispered.

"In the secret forest of Everlorn, in a hidden valley where no men have ever trod, grow the shendaaso, the

Flowers of Sleep. They thrive on the dreams of men and I have given you their petals, crushed with melted snow from the Ultimate Mountains. Drink and sleep."

Forollkin drank and Elmandis' face, the painted ceiling and the figure of Kerish dissolved into a swirl of colour. At the centre was something dark and huge, something that grew like a vast purple-black flower, folding back its petals. In the middle of the pulsing darkness a speck of light increased until it seemed a gaping hole in the firmament. The world tilted and Forollkin fell down and down into an endless well of light.

Elmandis put down the first chalice and took the second.

"Prince, you may not watch any further. Walk wherever you wish in Tir-Rinnon and return in three hours. Your brother is safe in the cradle of sleep, I promise you."

As Kerish went out he glimpsed Elmandis leaning over Forollkin with an expression on his face of intense concentration or, perhaps, of pain.

Kerish wandered disconsolately around the palace garden till he was approached by a man whose face he remembered from the Place of Fountains.

"I am Soreas," he announced. "If you haven't eaten, Kerish, I should be honoured to welcome you into my house to share our meal."

The Prince stared at him in astonishment at such familiarity. Mistaking the cause of his hesitation, Soreas said warmly: "Truly it will be no trouble. Do come. We so rarely see strangers in Tir-Rinnon."

Kerish remembered his manners and his hunger.

"Thank you . . . Soreas. I would be honoured to come."

The Ellerinionn led Kerish to a white house on the edge of the city, built around a small but beautiful garden. A shady colonnade ran round the inside of the house and cushions had been set there and a table laid for a meal. First, however, Soreas showed his guest the whole house and especially a ceiling that he had just finished painting. The design was a circle of leaping fish and grotesque sea monsters around a tree of coral and Kerish exclaimed in delight at the vibrant colours and lively creatures. He asked how long it had taken to complete.

"The painting itself no more than five days," said Soreas, "but of course I sketched for it and thought about it for weeks."

"And you have the time to paint like this often?"

"Always. When we are in Ellerinonn our only duty is to our art."

"Is everyone here an artist?" asked Kerish incredulously.

"Of some kind, yes." Soreas smiled. "I suppose that must seem strange to you."

"Not entirely," answered Kerish, tilting back his head to look at the ceiling again. "In Galkis all the nobles are taught to write and play and sing and dance, and craftsmen are held in the greatest honour because the Book of the Emperors says that 'to create is to mirror the action of God'."

"We have no gods here," said Soreas lightly. "Elmandis has freed us from them."

He led Kerish into the colonnade and they sat down among the scattered cushions. A blonde child ran through the garden carrying garlands of fresh blue flowers. She put one round Kerish's neck, gave the other to Soreas and then climbed on his lap to hug him.

"This is my daughter Reahno."

A plump young man and a curly-haired woman came towards them carrying baskets of fruit. They also received garlands from Reahno.

"And here is my sister Ideao and her husband Gannius. They live in the Valley of Shining Streams, some distance from Tir-Rinnon, but they are staying with me while my wife is Beyond."

"Otherwise he would waste away," explained Ideao. "Soreas is so absorbed in his painting he never remembers to gather fruit for himself."

Kerish was presented with a bowl of fresh fruit and a fine porcelain cup of fragrant wine.

"The fruit on the trees is for everyone to pick?"

"Oh yes, indeed," answered Gannius, "and by the grace of Elmandis there is always enough."

"More than enough," said Soreas with mock gravity. "If we did not stop you, brother, you would eat sweet jellahns till you burst."

"Don't believe him," protested Gannius, with his mouth full. "Of course I pick them to copy in the patterns on my plates and jars. I'm a potter, Kerish, and naturally they'd rot if I didn't eat them . . . which would be wasteful . . ."

The rest of the explanation was lost in the others' laughter. Not at all abashed, Gannius offered Kerish a jellahn. It was curiously shaped, with a skin mottled in lurid shades of red and purple, but it tasted delicious.

"Did I understand that your wife is abroad?" asked Kerish.

Soreas frowned. "Yes. From time to time we must all leave Ellerinonn to work in the dark places of the world as teachers or healers, but it is not our custom to talk about it, or about those who are Beyond."

Kerish began to apologize but the little girl had followed the conversation.

"Father, you said Mother would be back for my birthday. Why didn't she come?"

"She was needed, Reahno."

"I don't want to go away to the cruel places!"

"Reahno, that is enough." Soreas pushed her from his lap. "Now go and bring a finger bowl for our guest."

When the brief meal was over they sat around a lily pond in the centre of the garden finishing their wine. Ideao asked Kerish if he would like to hear a song and she had soon fetched and tuned her lyre. She sang of her home in the Valley of Shining Streams to a tune that leaped and sparkled like the waterfalls. Then Kerish himself was teased into admitting his talents. Ideao found an instrument for him that was very like a zildar. He tuned it cautiously, played a few chords and then, without knowing why, launched into the last song that the Poet Emperor ever wrote, "Come, gentle death, and lead me from the dark." It was in High Galkian so the Ellerinionns could not understand the words but they all seemed moved by the sweet melancholy of its music.

Soreas himself stared into the pool and hardly spoke again, while Kerish and the others discussed music, until it was time to take the Prince back to the palace.

In the Chamber of Healing Forollkin slept and Elmandis still held the golden chalice.

"You have been longer than I said," he murmured as Kerish came in; "you must have been happy."

"My Lord, how is Forollkin?"

Elmandis smiled. "In a moment you shall ask him yourself. Help me now."

Kerish lifted Forollkin's head while Elmandis held the chalice to the young Galkian's lips and forced a few drops down his throat. Forollkin stirred, coughed, and opened his eyes.

"I saw them growing," he muttered, "flowers, huge and black..."

Elmandis set down the chalice and shook him by the shoulders. "Return."

Forollkin blinked and sat up, fully awake.

"Kerish. Majesty... I don't remember how..."

Elmandis stepped back. "Look at your leg now."

Forollkin did and gasped. Where the wound had been was smooth brown skin without a mark. Forollkin prodded the place as if he could not believe the evidence of his eyes.

"Do you believe in the power of the Seven Sorcerers now?" asked Elmandis.

Forollkin stretched and bent his leg. "I suppose I must," he said ungraciously. "I thank your Majesty."

"You must try out your leg, of course, before believing," murmured Elmandis. "In the cool of the evening young people gather outside my palace to run and throw and wrestle. Join them and tonight I shall hold a banquet in your honour."

"Your Majesty, the captain of the *Zeloka*..." began Forollkin.

"Worthy Engis has already been told that you will not return till morning," said Elmandis, "and some of my people have gone of their own accord to feast the crew."

"Lord King, I must speak to you alone," murmured Kerish.

"After the banquet, Prince."

135

Kerish and Forollkin joined a group of bronzed Ellerinionns on a wide, green lawn. Forollkin wrestled and Kerish
was caught up in a game of toss ball. In Galkis he had often
enviously watched young soldiers play this very game.
Now there was no one to forbid a royal Prince to join
undignified pursuits and he leaped and tossed joyfully.

After the sports they bathed with the Ellerinionns in an
indoor pool fed by a warm spring, and were then led to a
pleasant room overlooking a walled garden. They dried
themselves and, with some difficulty, dressed in the clothes
that had been laid out for them. These were lengths of fine
white linen bordered with spirals and rosettes, woven in
red and blue. Forollkin felt most uneasy and insisted on
pinning his at the waist, but the simple folds suited his lean
body and sun-darkened skin.

Footsteps sounded on marble and Soreas stood smiling
in the doorway. Kerish greeted him with pleasure and
introduced Forollkin. The Ellerinionn grasped Forollkin's
hand.

"We are glad to see you healed. Elmandis wishes me to
take you to the Place of Feasting and my daughter sends
you these."

He gave them bracelets skilfully made from red and blue
flowers stitched on to bands of cloth.

"Tonight they are beautiful, tomorrow they will be
faded," said Soreas. "These are the jewels of Ellerinonn."

"And do you not care for cold, eternal gems?" asked
Kerish.

Soreas answered him gravely, "We care only for things
that remind us of our humanity. The flowers come again
each year. New flowers and new men to receive our heritage."

"Don't you believe in a life after death?" demanded
Forollkin.

"No," said Soreas, "Elmandis has taught us to live
without such a hope, and we are the stronger for it. Will
you come?"

The Place of Feasting was a courtyard paved in creamy
marble and surrounded by pillared terraces. The feasting
area was lit by torches held in the pale stone hands of

statues of generations of young Ellerinionns. The terraces were scattered with brightly woven cushions and low couches had been placed round the edge of a dancing floor. Already the place was full of people, deep in earnest conversations or tuning instruments.

Soreas led the Galkians to where Elmandis reclined, a crown of flowers overshadowing his face. The King asked them to share his couch, Kerish on his right and Forollkin on his left. Soreas then joined his family on the other side of the dancing floor.

As soon as they were seated, children ran up with baskets of flowers. Elmandis plucked out a crimson wreath and placed it on Kerish's head. The flowers brought back too vividly the soft voice of the Emperor, a crimson cup and a dead woman. Kerish sat very still trying to shut out the memory. Elmandis clapped his hands for the feasting to begin. Rare fruits, sugared flowers, bread, honey and bowls of soft cheese and yoghurt were brought.

The feasters sat in small groups sharing woven baskets of fruit and painted chalices of wine or nectar. As they ate Ellerinionns strolled on to the dancing floor to entertain the company. Some danced, lightly and gracefully, their white robes rippling like the sea, some played lutes and lyres, some sang and some recited poetry.

In compliment to their guests, a group chanted a Galkian hymn known through all Zindar, "Oh Golden Galkis, matchless star of cities, beneath the snow-clad mountains ever shining..." When it was over Kerish was asked to sing or play.

Kerish took a draught of wine, nervously tuned a borrowed instrument and sang the Lay of Prince Tor-Koldin and the White Trieldiss. In his pure, flawless voice, he told how five hundred years before, the Trieldiss, the rarest of beasts, had appeared in the mountains above Galkis. Whoever ate its heart would become a great poet, and that above all Tor-Koldin desired. His thoughts sparkled like fire jewels but when he tried to catch them on paper their beauty faded. The young Prince took the bow and arrows forbidden to the Godborn and went up into the mountains. For seven days he followed the Trieldiss as it leapt from crag to crag and at last he brought it to bay against a wall of rock. For the first time he saw the beast clearly and it was beautiful beyond his imagining. He could not destroy such perfection even for his heart's desire. He threw down his bow and sadly turned away but to his wonder the Trieldiss spoke.

"Prince Tor-Koldin, you have spared my beauty, you have a poet's soul, and with it my heart."

The Prince returned to the Golden City and set down in words the beauty of the Trieldiss and he became the Poet Emperor, famous in Zindar as the greatest who ever expressed the thoughts and feelings of men.

Kerish had chosen well. His song delighted the Ellerin-ionns and even Elmandis smiled at the Prince and shared with him his cup of nectar. A lively circle dance began and a laughing, fair-haired girl caught Forollkin by the hand and made him join them. They would have taken Kerish too but Elmandis shook his head.

"If you would speak with me alone, come with me now."

Kerish nodded and he followed Elmandis as he strode away from the music and light and laughter into the darkness.

Chapter 10

The Book of the Emperors: *Warnings*
Remember that God sees every action of your life and knows
each thought. There is no abyss dark enough to hide from his
light.

ELMANDIS led Kerish down a passage in which no
torches burned, and unlocked a black door that opened
on to a small, circular chamber. While the King lit an alabaster lamp, Kerish looked around him. The walls were
hung with seven panels each bearing a life-sized image: no,
not seven but six, for the last panel was cracked and
darkened as if it had gone through fire.

The first was a portrait of Elmandis, the second of a fair
boy very like him. The third was a silver-haired woman;
the others were harder to make out, for as Kerish stared at
the portraits they seemed to sink below the shadowy
surface of the panels and vanish.

The seventh at first seemed to bear no image but as
Kerish looked at it closely the darkness appeared to swirl
and shift and from its depths floated up a white face. White
as stripped bone and riven as if by a terrible blow, between
the glittering eyes. Kerish shuddered and tried to look
away. To his horror he could not, the eyes held him.

Kerish stumbled backwards and cried out: "No!"

Elmandis looked up, strode forward and struck his hand
across the panel. It became nothing but dark, cracked glass
again.

The image of the riven face was still imprinted on
Kerish's eyes. Elmandis gently called his name and held the
tips of his fingers against Kerish's eyelids. The Prince
swayed a little and sat down in an ebony chair.

"What was it?" Kerish asked.

"One drowned in darkness far deeper than *my* power could reach. Yet you could raise him..."

Elmandis looked curiously at Kerish, then pounced on the cirge chain about his neck and drew out the purple jewel.

"Prince, do you know what you wear at your heart?"

"It was the gift of the High Priest of Zeldin," said Kerish.

"Then if good Izeldon did not choose to tell you I will not; but it was a great gift, and enough to draw Shubeyash to you."

"Shubeyash?"

"The King of Roac, the Lord of the Restless Dead," said Elmandis. "Once there were seven sorcerers, now there are six."

"He was a sorcerer, he held a key?" asked Kerish eagerly.

"He holds it still with all his power. Will you challenge the walking dead, Prince of Galkis?"

"I will challenge all the Seven Sorcerers," answered Kerish solemnly, "for I must win their keys to free the Saviour. Lord Elmandis, only you can help me."

"I do not wish to help you," said Elmandis coldly.

"Why, why?"

Elmandis circled the room, never looking at the Prince. "I will tell you as much as I may. My people believe that my power is the summit of what can be achieved by the human mind. That is a half truth. The labours of my mind brought me to a state of knowledge equalled only by six others in the history of Zindar. That knowledge brought each of us to make a bargain with the one you Galkians call Zeldin. I cannot tell you all the terms of that bargain but the centre of it was this: each of us was given a golden key to guard. So long as we hold those keys we are immortal; so long and not a moment longer. If I give up my key I will begin to age. In due time I will die and the power that protects Ellerinonn will die with me.

"No, don't speak yet," said Elmandis rapidly. "When the others received their keys they were grateful. I railed

140

against even so slight a limit to my power. Zeldin rewarded my ingratitude: he gave me a second key, a key of knowledge. Without that knowledge no one could win the keys to the Saviour's prison and so the fate of the Seven Sorcerers is locked within my mind."

"Lord Elmandis, you have already begun to unlock that knowledge for me . . ."

"Perhaps I do so only to torment you?"

"Your people do not speak of you as a tyrant," said Kerish.

"Is that not the final proof of my tyranny?"

Elmandis laughed and Kerish's hands clasped nervously on the Jewel of Zeldin.

"I think you are wrong to teach your people to live without a god," he said, "but you do it out of love for them, so I know that you must understand Zeldin's love for you."

"I understand it," agreed Elmandis. "The weight of his love down all these centuries begins to suffocate me."

"Lord, if he loves you surely no evil could come to you or Ellerinonn from giving up the key," began Kerish, "for that is what he always intended. Surely he will protect Ellerinonn?"

"Did he protect your crew from the Brigands?"

Kerish flinched and Elmandis stopped his pacing and stood for a moment facing the darkened panel.

"Forgive me, that was cruel and it would be fair to throw my words back at me. I have no doubt that Zeldin would act for the good of my people but I wish to control their destiny and mine. I called you proud because I saw in you a faint image of myself."

"Lord Elmandis, surely the only way to keep your pride is to submit to Zeldin of your own free will. Izeldon told me that. I couldn't accept it," admitted Kerish, "but perhaps you will take it from me."

"Perhaps I will . . ."

Elmandis sat down in a chair opposite Kerish and studied the Prince's face: "But if I am to gamble my pride on you, what will stand surety?"

The Sorcerer's sea-green eyes were like waves poised to

141

break over the Prince and Kerish looked down at his hands.

"Even if I give you my knowledge and my key," murmured Elmandis, "you have a terrible journey still to make and keys to win from six unwilling sorcerers. How can I believe that you will ever achieve your quest?"

"Lord Elmandis, you recognized me when you saw me," said the Prince. "Surely you knew from the beginning that it was I who would undertake this quest?"

"I have always known that it might be you, Kerish-lo-Taan," agreed the Enchanter, "but there were others among your kin who might have freed the Saviour. Their own choices barred them from the quest. With the power of my key I may look forward and see the choices that will confront you, but I cannot see your changing thoughts and feelings, so I have no certainty. I do not know you deeply enough."

"Perhaps if we stayed a while..." began Kerish eagerly.

"A while! It would require a life-time and you do not have my immortality. Don't look so desolate, Prince," said Elmandis softly, "there is a way. If you will let me I can look into your past and from that judge your future."

"Then do it," urged Kerish.

"You speak lightly; but you will need all your courage to spend one night in the Chamber of Seeing."

"Take me there," said Kerish-lo-Taan.

Forollkin soon noticed that Kerish was missing but was not disturbed. Someone told him that the King had taken Kerish to his own chamber to talk. Forollkin sat contentedly listening to the singers, musicians and poets, and sipping his wine till past midnight, when the torch dance began. Either arm grasped by a laughing Ellerinionn, he was whirled through gardens and orchards up into the hills to watch the sunrise. At dawn Forollkin returned drowsily to his room. Kerish was not there but a message was brought to say that he was sleeping in a nearby chamber. Forollkin thanked the messenger, rolled into bed and slept till an hour before noon.

While Forollkin was drinking and dancing, Kerish lay on a hard couch in the Chamber of Seeing. There were no windows in the chamber and Kerish heard Elmandis lock the single door behind him. Floor, walls and ceiling were carved with huge, closed eyes. A single lamp hung over the couch.

Kerish was almost afraid to settle, imagining that the moment he stopped looking at them the closed lids all around him would suddenly open. He lay staring up at the lamp, a dazzling light that swung gently from side to side; stared fascinated into the fiery depths, forgetting even the ominous eyes till the brilliance became unbearable. Kerish's lashed fluttered down and he slept.

Almost at once he was trapped in a vivid dream. He was still lying in the Chamber of Seeing but the room had changed horribly. The light of the lamp was gone. Instead the chamber was faintly lit by the green glare of a hundred eyes. They were all around him, veined with pulsing red, with green irises and black pupils, slit with yellow fire. Kerish tried to scream but the sound choked in his throat; he tried to move but was frozen to the couch. Yet even at so slight a movement the eyes swivelled round and gazed only at him.

Kerish knew they were not looking at his face. He felt the green glare strip away the skin, flesh and bone and lay bare his mind and memory. All the years, the days, the hours of his life were mercilessly exposed; every action he had ever taken; every word he had ever spoken. All the petty lies; all the small forgotten crimes; every thought or speech he had ever been ashamed of, came flooding into his mind and the eyes saw. The defences he had built up so carefully over the years were stripped away, leaving him naked.

He could not bear it. He knew that unless there was one place left in his mind where he could hide from the eyes, he would go mad under their pitiless gaze. Then from the mass of memories one image stood out. The face of his father, the face of the Godborn, and the Emperor's voice saying: "And this gift I give you, the cruel gift of seeing truth through the mists of illusion."

"I am in a dream," whispered Kerish; "this is only a nightmare."

But the eyes were all around him.

"Illusion, this is illusion." He tensed every muscle in his body and concentrated with the strength of desperation. "This is illusion. I am dreaming. I will wake!"

Kerish felt a stab of pain. The eyes closed, the darkness faded and he was looking up into the brilliance of the lamp. Kerish found that his hands were clutching the purple jewel so tightly that its facets had cut into his fingers. The pain had obviously woken him. The Prince sat up and looked around. The eyes were closed but he dared not lie down again. He knew that if he slept he would be lost in the same hideous nightmare and this time he might not have the strength to wake.

He leaped off the couch and ran to the door. It was still locked. He hammered at it but his hands seemed to make no sound.

"Zeldin, how many hours till dawn?" He could not know and he must keep awake.

With dragging feet Kerish paced round and round the silent chamber, his hands clutching painfully at the Jewel of Zeldin. Some four hours later Elmandis unlocked the door. Wide-eyed and pale, Kerish was leaning against the wall. They stared at each other for a moment. Kerish took a few steps toward the King, and quietly fainted.

The Prince woke just before noon. He sat up and stared at his unblemished hands and then tried to remember the reason for his surprise. The horror of the Chamber of Seeing came flooding back: the horror of failure.

Somehow he had said the right things to the Sorcerer but now that Elmandis knew what a despicable person he was, he would never win the key. There was a knock on the door and Soreas entered carrying a cup full to the brim with golden liquid. It was the same Blood of the Sun that Kerish had tasted in Zeldin's temple and he drank it gratefully.

"You must get up quickly," ordered Soreas. "Elmandis is waiting. It is rare that he commands instead of asks, but he has changed since you came here. Kerish, what have you done to him?"

"I don't know," said Kerish wearily.

Soreas helped the Prince to fold the length of white cloth correctly round his body and they left the room together without speaking another word.

The Ellerinionn led Kerish to a small, sunken garden, where a group of people were seated on the grass beside a stream. Elmandis himself was leaning over the bank, trailing a hand through the water, but Forollkin stood up a little unsteadily to greet his brother and Reahno ran towards him with garlands of fresh flowers. Ideao was softly playing her lyre and Gannius was setting out bowls of fruit. Forollkin came forward and hugged his startled brother.

"Kerish, I'm sorry. I'd forgotten till the King reminded me and I've had no opportunity to get you anything."

"What?"

"Kerish, happy birthday," said Forollkin simply.

He was joined by a chorus of good wishes but Kerish stared blankly. His birthday: he came of age today and he had forgotten. In Galkis it would have been an occasion for intricate ritual and costly celebration. Kerish returned his brother's hug with fervour.

Soreas was smiling now. "Come and see your presents."

"Presents?"

Reahno grabbed Kerish's hands and led him to his place on the bank. Beside a bowl of yellow and red fruit was a great heap of leaves and flowers.

"You must scrabble for them," explained Reahno.

Kerish knelt and swept away the top layer of leaves and petals to discover a scroll of exquisitely written Ellerinionn poems, a finely carved flute and a pottery flask made by Gannius and painted with winged circles, the Galkian symbol of the soul. Soreas had worked all morning to finish it.

The delight in the Prince's face amply repaid the givers, but suddenly Elmandis turned round and said:

"I wish you joy on your birthday, Kerish-lo-Taan. What gift can the King of Ellerinonn give to the Prince of Galkis?"

"My Lord, you know," murmured Kerish, not daring to look into the sea-green eyes.

Elmandis unclenched his left hand to reveal a slender golden key set with a purple gem and hanging from a golden chain.

"I wish you courage, also. Here is my gift. Take it if you can!"

Kerish stared at it for a moment and then at Elmandis' tortured face. He reached out for the key and in the second that he touched it, Kerish saw lovely Ellerinonn desolate. Tir-Rinnon was a ruin, its walls and columns cracked and fallen. Grass choked the courtyards and the fountains and half hid the broken slabs of bloodstained marble and the yellowing bones. Kerish's hands closed on the key and the vision was gone. The sun gleamed on beautiful Tir-Rinnon and there was something very like peace in Elmandis' eyes.

"Lord King," Kerish's voice shook a little, "I thank you for your great gift."

"Prince, the pain of receiving it will be greater than the pain of giving it. Do not thank me yet," said Elmandis coldly. "Now, let us break our fast and be happy while we can."

Kerish looped the golden chain around his waist. The Ellerinionns, who had been standing tensely during the Prince's exchange with their King, sat down on the grass and began passing round a cup of nectar and eating fruit from each other's bowls.

Forollkin started his own awkward thanks to Elmandis but the King cut him short.

"Lord Forollkin, I hope you will show your gratitude by granting me a favour."

"You have only to name it, your Majesty," said the Galkian.

Elmandis scooped up an amber fruit and began to peel it as he spoke.

"I do no more than ask. The favour may be greater than it seems. Will you take a travelling companion? I warn you, he has been soured by suffering and now only the strongest or the sweetest can digest his company. He came

146

to me asking for a spell to be performed. What that spell was you must never ask him."

Puzzled, the Galkians nodded their assent.

"I refused," continued Elmandis. "He then tried to reach the sorcerer of Tir-Racneth and failed. Now he waits in the Bay of Rindiss for a ship north. Kerish, promise me that he shall travel with you wherever you go."

"To the world's end!" said Kerish lightly.

"Prince, I will hold you to that, and may you never have cause to regret your promise," murmured Elmandis, a glimmer of amusement in his green eyes.

Forollkin wiped some juice from his mouth and said: "Lord King, you mentioned a sorcerer of Tir-Racneth..."

Soreas, who was sitting next to Forollkin, jabbed him with his elbow as if he had said something dangerous but Elmandis answered calmly:

"Ellandellore, Lord of Tir-Racneth ... you must visit him tomorrow, Prince. The key at your waist unlocks the casket of the second key."

"What must I do?" asked Kerish.

"We will sail together through the Straits of Rac but you alone must visit Cheransee, the Isle of Illusions, and confront Ellandellore."

"The two of us alone," said Forollkin stolidly.

"No, the danger to you would be too great," announced the King. "Ellandellore is a master of illusion and capricious as a wilful child. He would destroy you, my worthy soldier."

"If it is too dangerous for me it is too dangerous for Kerish!" protested Forollkin.

"Not so. Kerish has the gifts of the Godborn."

Elmandis delved into his bowl and then opened his hand.

"Forollkin, what do you see?"

"A fruit: a round, reddish-brown fruit."

"And you Soreas, Gannius, Ideao?" They answered in chorus: "The same."

"Though I would have said it was more purplish-brown than red," added Ideao.

Reahno opened her mouth to say something but was nudged into silence by her father.

Elmandis shook his hand.

"Do you hear the seeds rattling, Forollkin?"

"Yes."

"Taste it then," suggested Elmandis.

Cautiously, Forollkin took a bite. He grimaced and tried to spit it out but there was nothing in his mouth but a foul taste and nothing in his hand.

"You would starve in an orchard of such fruits," said Elmandis with a grim smile. "Kerish, what did you see?"

"A ball of mist in your hand, nothing more."

"Good. Forollkin, Kerish's eyes will see through the mists of Cheransee where yours would betray you."

"If they're only illusions they might frighten me but they won't hurt me," said Forollkin stubbornly.

"Fear always has the power to hurt," answered Elmandis. "The fruit tasted bitter to you; I could have made you think yourself poisoned. Cheransee is an island of nightmares and you cannot save yourself by waking up, for you are not asleep."

"But nightmares still aren't real," persisted Forollkin.

"Reality is different for each man," answered Elmandis. "One believes in the power of a swamp sorcerer and dies under his curse, another does not and laughs at his gibberings. Is the sorcerer's power real or unreal? While you think of a reply, Lord Forollkin, we will walk to the harbour."

Captain Engis hastily discarded his garland and flowery bracelets as the Prince came aboard. He and his crew knelt.

"Captain," Kerish took Engis by the arm and raised him up, "I think for the rest of the voyage we will dispense with such formalities."

"As your Highness pleases," stammered Engis, and he bowed to the King of Ellerinonn and saluted Forollkin.

"Captain, we wish to sail through the Straits of Rac to Rindiss Bay. Can we make a start today?" asked Kerish, "or do you need more time to provision?"

"By the King's kindness we are well provisioned," answered the Captain gratefully. "We could reach Thilik by nightfall and there's good anchorage there."

"Thank you, Captain Engis."

The crew went speedily to work and Soreas and his family, who had carried Kerish's gifts down to the ship, prepared to leave. They all embraced him and wished him good fortune.

"Perhaps in your travels you will meet my wife," said Soreas. "Her name is Leahno. If you find her tell her that Ellerinonn is not complete while she is Beyond."

"I will."

Kerish waved at the Ellerinionns as they ran down the gangplank and Elmandis whispered: "Leahno ... she died two months ago in the dungeons of Orze."

Kerish forced himself to continue smiling as the wind sprang at the *Zeloka's* sails and dragged her out to sea.

The Prince offered his cabin to Elmandis but the King refused.

"I have no need of sleep. I will stay here."

From sunset to dawn he stood silently by the figurehead and the crew crept round him, more afraid to look at his face than at their Prince.

Kerish slept badly that night. A dozen times he dreamed that he was back in the Chamber of Seeing, beating on the door, trying to escape from the eyes. In his terror he cried out to Elmandis, and he seemed to see the King standing on the starlit deck and to hear his calm voice. Then he was no longer afraid and sank back into quiet sleep.

Once, at the end of the long night, he had a different dream. In the darkness of his cabin he saw his father crouching by an alabaster sarcophagus. Laughing, the Emperor dragged off the lid and reached in.

"No! I won't look at her, I won't."

Kerish struggled against the dream and woke. He sat up and looked around the empty cabin as the pale, grey light of dawn came creeping through the window. There was no dawn in Kerish's mind and longing for human company, he dressed and went on deck. Elmandis met him with a cup of shining liquid.

"Drink, you will need your strength today."

Kerish drained the cup and sat down on the couch

beneath the dew-sodden awning.

"I have filled the flask that Soreas painted for you with the Blood of the Sun," added Elmandis. "Take it on your journey and use it sparingly. Perhaps it will be of more use to your companions than to you. You have drunk enough to strengthen an army and look no better for it."

"I'm not used to getting up at dawn, that's all," said Kerish sulkily.

Elmandis sat down beside him.

"I would have thought that one whose dreams were haunted would be glad to rise early. We pay the penalty for seeing through illusion, we know that we are alone in the darkness of reality. Don't pity me, Prince," commanded Elmandis. "That is one thing I forbid both to my subjects and my guests."

Captain Engis, who had been steering the *Zeloka* through the dawn mists, left the tiller and bowed to the Prince and the King.

"My Lords, will you eat? It's a cold morning; perhaps some spiced wine and a dish of kardiss will warm you."

Elmandis courteously refused but Kerish thanked the captain for his timely thought.

"Oh, and would you ask Lord Forollkin to join us."

Forollkin soon came yawning on to deck and saluted the King.

"Lord Elmandis, can you tell us more about this sorcerer of Tir-Racneth?"

After a long silence the King replied:

"Ellandellore of Tir-Racneth is great in power, but he has the mind of a mischievous child. He is wilful and cruel, yet quick to cry. You cannot reason with him, Kerish. You must treat him as you would a child and play his games, remembering that he has the strength to carry out his petulant threats."

"My Lord, do you think he will give me his key?" asked Kerish.

"I do not know. He might destroy you merely for asking, or he might trade his greatest treasure for a pretty pebble." Elmandis frowned. "His moods change as quickly as water in the wind."

"Could you not tame him, Lord Elmandis?" demanded Forollkin.

"No. By the Law of the Seven no sorcerer may set foot in another's territory, without their permission. It is a wise law framed to preserve Zindar from our quarrels and I will not break it," declared the King. "You and I, Forollkin, must wait for Kerish in Rindiss Bay."

Two crewmen arrived with the food and wine. Forollkin gratefully shovelled down the steaming kardiss as Kerish sat shivering.

"Come on, eat," said his brother cheerfully; "you can't face a sorcerer on an empty stomach."

Kerish picked up his bowl.

"And you're shivering like grass in the wind. Here, take my cloak."

He wrapped it round the Prince's shoulders.

"Fasten it then!"

"Forollkin, please leave me alone!"

Kerish slammed down the bowl and stalked to the rail, his back to the world.

As Forollkin scooped up the discarded cloak, Elmandis lightly touched his shoulder.

"There is nothing you can do to help him."

"But he is so afraid, so helpless."

"No, Forollkin, he is not and if you mock his strength too often he will turn it on you," warned Elmandis.

"I don't mock him. The Emperor and the High Priest told me to protect Kerish," said Forollkin doggedly, "and I will."

The pale sun of early morning glinted on the purple sails. The mists were clearing. Behind the *Zeloka* the sea was calm and to starboard stretched the gentle coast of Ellerinonn, but ahead there was the angry sound of waves shattering on rocks and the sight of the great wall of fog that always hid the Isle of Cheransee.

The barren coast of Mintaz and fair Ellerinonn were separated by a channel some ten miles wide. Between the two countries lay the sorcerer's island and the straits were filled with a maze of rock, hidden just below the surface. There was only a narrow passage on either side of Cheransee through which ships could pass.

As the *Zeloka* sailed abreast of the island, Kerish joined Engis at the tiller.

"If any ship tries to pass these straits without paying tribute to the sorcerer," said the captain, "he sends down storms or mists. There's many a vessel been torn apart on these rocks and all her men drowned through the Lord of Tir-Racneth's anger."

A winding trail of smooth purple sea marked the safe water. On either side of it the waves frothed as they struck the unseen rocks. The *Zeloka* moved cautiously forward and the captain was soon too intent on steering to talk to Kerish. The Prince crossed to where Forollkin and Elmandis stood at the rail looking at the remains of a proud ship of Gilaz impaled on the inner rocks.

"Not all those who die here are the victims of Ellandellore," said the King softly. "Many ships are lost by careless captains before they come to the Place of Tribute."

"Could he not save them?" asked Forollkin.

"Perhaps. He is not cruel by nature. He sees a ship in the distance and thinks of it as a toy. He watches it sink, judges it a pretty game and then cries because his toy cannot be mended to sail and sink again."

"But to use people as toys . . ." began Forollkin.

"Blame those who taught him," said Elmandis harshly, "not the child."

The sun rose in the sky but Cheransee was still shrouded in mist. For three hours the *Zeloka* was borne swiftly forward by a strong current. Then the current slackened. The strip of safe water vanished and ahead loomed a barrier of rocks, showing black above the spray. The anchor was lowered to keep the *Zeloka* from drifting against the rocks and Engis left the tiller.

"This is the Place of Tribute, your Highness. We must wait here."

It was not long before a dim, black shape emerged from the mist. Kerish's keen eyes soon saw that it was a boat without sail or mast and carved like a sea monster. The boat was quite empty, yet it moved swiftly towards the

Zeloka. Engis attached a rope to a chest of coins and trinkets and lowered it down into the black boat as soon as it came alongside. When the rope came up again, Elmandis told Kerish to tie it around his own waist.

Engis began to protest but the King continued calmly:

"Prince, you must let this boat carry you to the shores of Cheransee. The sorcerer will sense your presence and it will not be difficult to find him. If you persuade him to give you his key, you must leave the island at once. To make the boat obey you, put your mouth to the figurehead and speak these words." He stooped to whisper them in Kerish's ear.

"Do you understand?"

The Prince nodded but Forollkin said:

"Kerish, I am coming with you. Lord Elmandis, this is a Galkian ship and you may not command me here. Kerish!"

The Prince had already knotted the rope around his waist and was swinging himself up on to the ship's rail. Forollkin took two steps towards him but Elmandis' hands clamped down on his shoulders. Coldness crippled Forollkin, his limbs froze and refused to obey his frantic thoughts. Kerish smiled faintly at his brother and ordered Engis to lower him down into the black boat. The captain hesitated and was caught in Elmandis' green gaze. Trembling suddenly, he summoned his men and Kerish disappeared over the side of the ship.

The black boat rocked as Kerish was lowered into it. He knelt, gripping the sides for balance, and then undid the rope at his waist with shaking fingers. He watched it spiral upwards as the crew drew it back. Beneath him the black boat shuddered.

Elmandis released Forollkin and he slumped to the deck. Engis rushed forward and rubbed warmth back into his limbs. Leaning against the captain, Forollkin made his way to the rail. He saw the black boat vanishing into the mist, with Kerish sitting at the prow, his face towards Cheransee.

"Captain, the way ahead is clear now," said Elmandis.

"Sail on."

Engis glanced at Forollkin who nodded helplessly. The anchor was drawn up and Forollkin fumbled among his thoughts to shape a prayer to Zeldin. Elmandis understood.

"Yes, pray. It is all either of us can do, now I have released my prisoner and become human. Pray for them both."

"Both?"

"For Kerish, because he alone can preserve Ellerinonn," said the King, "and for Ellandellore, because he is my brother."

Kerish looked ahead to the mountain of mist that was Cheransee and beneath him the black boat throbbed like a live thing. He hated having to touch it but he was grateful for the speed and skill with which the boat skimmed the waves, heedless of the rocks beneath. One scrape against those jagged rocks, one tear in the hull and he would drown, but the black boat made no mistake and sped on towards the sorcerer's island.

Kerish felt for the key at his waist and fingered it, still only half believing that Elmandis had given away the source of his power. But suppose he had not? Suppose he was in league with the sorcerer of Tir-Racneth and had sent him here to die? Kerish tried to stifle the thought by telling himself how glad he was to be free of Forollkin's scolding and interference. It rang hollow, and Kerish glanced back at the *Zeloka*. She was sailing serenely westwards under a sunlit sky.

Suddenly the black boat plunged into the wall of mist. It rapidly became very cold and Kerish was glad that he had put on his warmest Galkian clothes. He could only see a few feet ahead but he guessed from the sound of the waves breaking that he was near the shore. Something vast and black loomed ahead, an archway of naked rock towering above a cauldron of white water. The boat was dragged swiftly towards it. Kerish shrank down, praying his craft would not smash against the rock. For a moment there was darkness and then pale, sickly light again.

154

The boat was swept straight through the archway and crunched against the shore, sending the Prince sprawling onto the boards. When the black timbers had ceased to quiver, Kerish sat up and looked around him. There was still no trace of the bright sun that had lit the *Zeloka*. Above Cheransee the sky was colourless and dreary mist floated in straggling patches or crawled along the ground. All Kerish could see was a mile or more of flat, grey sand and beyond that something dark and tall.

Shivering, Kerish climbed out of the boat and sank up to his ankles in wet sand. The craft he had disliked so much now seemed a lone friend in this desolate place. Reluctantly he let go of the smooth timber and began to walk towards the distant darkness.

The crossing of the beach seemed interminable. In the grey sand that stuck to Kerish's clothes and sucked at his heels, there was no driftwood, no seaweed, no shells, no sign at all of sea life. Sometimes thick drifts of mist enveloped the Prince and he had to grope his way forward, careful always to keep the sound of the sea behind him.

As the crashing of the waves grew fainter he began to hear new sounds. They were still far in the distance but they left Kerish standing trembling for minutes at a time before he could nerve himself to go on. There were cries, shrieks and laughter from the darkness ahead. The cries of the lost and lonely; the shrieks of the tormented; and tainted laughter. A shroud of mist clung to him and he could see nothing.

Kerish-lo-Taan opened the front of his tunic and drew out the Jewel of Zeldin. Holding it in his right hand he edged forward. The High Priest's gift did nothing to dispel the thickening mist but it gave Kerish the courage he needed to keep moving.

Robbed of sight, his other senses seemed heightened. He felt the texture of the sand squelching beneath his boots as if he were barefoot and heard the sound of his own breath and heartbeat and, suddenly, from close by, a wailing scream. Kerish stumbled forward and his hands touched something dank and cold. The scream sounded again. Kerish dropped to his knees and hid his face in his hands like a child afraid of the dark.

After a long spell of utter silence the Prince forced himself to stand up and open his eyes. The mists were clearing. He stood beneath a huge rock twisted into the shape of a winged beast. Kerish stepped back a few paces. In either direction stretched a line of towering rocks, grotesquely shaped like giants and monsters. All were hideous, as if in the morning of the world some cruel creator had moulded them in the patterns of his diseased fancy. Yet they were only rocks, streaked with slime and crumbling with age.

"Rocks cannot hurt me," murmured Kerish. "They can't move; they can't speak and if they seem to, it will be nothing but illusion."

Even so, he found that he was whispering as if he were afraid the rocks would overhear and prove him wrong.

"Illusion!" he repeated more firmly, and ducked under a lifeless claw to enter a maze of stone in which he was no bigger than an ant in a cornfield. Hundreds of terrible shapes blocked out the light and Kerish wandered in a dim underworld of black rock and floating mists.

He soon stopped trying to make out the towering shapes: the snarl on one vast face, the half-open beak and coiled tongue of a second and the clawed hands of a third shape frightened him too badly. Kerish began to feel that the moment he turned his back on them the rocks would move, darkness would tower above him and then descend to crush the life of one of the hated children of the gods who arrogantly called the earth their own.

To distract himself Kerish began to sing, randomly wandering from war chants to hymns, from ballads of love to children's rhymes. It gave him courage but he soon wished he had never opened his lips for his voice seemed to stir the brooding horror of the place. From shadows black as the Well of Time, and shapes mercifully shrouded in mist, came distant shrieks of torment, sobbing screams of despair and shattered laughter to echo round and round the rocks. If the rocks could speak . . . how often Kerish had heard that phrase. Here they could, and they spoke of ancient agonies and hate.

The Prince stared wildly round but in the darkness and mist nothing seemed to move, no giant mouths gaped in the rock. Kerish pressed his hands over his ears but he could not stop the cries echoing in his head. Abruptly Kerish's endurance snapped. He had to escape from the noise and stupidly he began to run. The white mist swooped down to blind him. He groped his way, catching at sharp and slippery rocks. Over and over again he whispered: "It's not real, it's not real!" And suddenly there was silence and Kerish's hands touched something different. A smooth, flat surface, dry and cold.

A gust of wind, the first he had felt on Cheransee, tore the mists away. In the dim light, Kerish stood facing a young man dressed in purple and gold. The shock of seeing a human again made Kerish step back and cry out:

"Who are you?"

There was no answer. He stared at the young man's face; a haunting face with foam-white skin stretched tightly over delicate bones, a face framed by shining, black hair, streaked with silver; but the eyes ... huge, inhuman, purple and gold and black, the eyes of the Godborn!

Kerish looked down at the rest of the figure. The young man's slim form was dressed in Galkian clothes and round his neck hung a brilliant purple gem on a cirge chain. Only then did Kerish realize that for the first time in his life he was looking at his own reflection.

"No!" Kerish recoiled in shock. "No! That isn't me. No!"

Kerish suddenly struggled to be free of his body like a bird beating against the bars of its cage. The Prince of the Godborn knew that he was within a fraction of remembering his history, and that his being stretched back to the darkness before creation.

Why did people call him Kerish? That was meaningless and this weak body that he now saw from the outside, restricted his power, his freedom ...

In answer to some frantic mental warning, Kerish had just enough strength to stop gazing into his own eyes. He spun round and found his hands up against a second cold wall of glass. He was trapped. To every side and above and

157

below there were mirrors. From every angle his reflection leaped out at him and on his own face was a cruel mocking smile. Kerish shouted:

"No, let me go!"

He threw himself at the wall of mirrors. The glass shattered. For a moment he thought his soul had escaped and he was flying up out of the blackness. Then the world seemed to tilt and for a few seconds he lost consciousness. He woke bewildered, and grieved about something he could not remember.

He was lying on grass. Kerish opened his eyes. High above him the sky was clear and blue.

Kerish sat up and found himself on the slope of a hill overlooking a pleasant grey-green island, walled with mist. At the summit of the hill was a tall, slender tower. It was built in pale blue stone and curved and twisted impossibly as it rose. Dozens of brilliantly-coloured banners and flags streamed in the breeze from its battlements or hung from star and moon-shaped windows lit from within and sending shafts of silvery light to challenge the sun. Kerish stared at it dizzily until a voice behind him said:

"Welcome, Prince, to Tir-Racneth."

Kerish swivelled round. Beside him on the grass sat a young boy who looked about nine or ten years old. Like Elmandis, he had copper skin and hair so fair it was almost white, but his eyes were green and wild. The boy was dressed in trailing lengths of splendid but tattered cloth, some sewn with jewels, some stained with salt water. He had a crown but it was too big and kept slipping down over his forehead.

"Ellandellore?"

The sorcerer of Tir-Racneth giggled.

"No, I am the Emperor of the Screaming Rocks. Can't you see my crown?"

Kerish got up and bowed.

"Pardon me, your Majesty, the sunlight dazzled me and I was blind."

Ellandellore smiled.

"I know who you are because of your eyes. You're the Prince of Galkis, and there's something I ought to remember about you but I don't know what. I saw your ship from my tower. I thought I might wreck her, but I didn't because she was pretty. You didn't like my subjects, the Screaming Rocks, did you? To tell you the truth," said Ellandellore in a confidential whisper, "I don't like them either, but I dream them every night and they won't go away. You didn't like the mirrors. The Godborn are afraid of mirrors, Elmandis told me."

"Elmandis?"

"Yes, my brother. He's older than me and very wise. He used to tell me his secrets but then he got angry and said I mustn't play the games I like, so I don't let him come here any more."

Kerish sat down again, trying not to appear as startled as he felt.

"Aren't you lonely here?"

"Oh yes, sometimes, but now I have you to play with."

"For a while," said Kerish cautiously.

The sorcerer of Tir-Racneth lay back on the grass, staring at the bright blue sky.

"Sometimes when the ships sink I send the Black Boat to fetch people, but humans aren't good at my games. They get frightened . . . but of course you know. You're half human."

He twisted his head to stare at the Prince.

"Ellandellore," said Kerish softly, "I will play any game you like if you will give me a small present."

The sorcerer laughed.

"Oh, but I can make you play because if you don't I'll shut you in my cage of mirrors . . . what sort of present?"

"Oh something that you have no use for, a small golden casket."

Ellandellore nodded gravely.

"Yes, I keep it in my tower. I keep it very safe. Elmandis said I must."

"I see. Well of course you must do what your brother tells you," said Kerish cunningly. "He always knows best."

Ellandellore sat up and spoke indignantly:

"No! I'll do what I like. I don't care what Elmandis says. People think he's clever but he's always sad and tired because of his silly humans and his precious Ellerinonn. That's stupid. I am wise. I am powerful. I am the Emperor of the Screaming Rocks and the Lord of Tir-Racneth. I do what I please and nobody stops me. That's what it means to be an Emperor, and I'm richer than Elmandis, much richer, shall I show you?"

The temptation to treat Ellandellore like a spoiled child and tell him to behave was very strong, but Kerish smiled encouragingly and said:

"Yes, I would be honoured."

In great excitement the sorcerer seized Kerish's wrist and led him through the door of the twisted tower.

Occupying the whole of the ground floor was the treasure chamber of Ellandellore, crammed with the spoils of hundreds of ships. In fabulous confusion gaping chests were piled to the ceiling: statues, lamps and swords were jumbled on the floor, lengths of Kolgorn silk, and cloth of gold for an Emperor's coronation lay in rotting heaps; jars of rare spices and unguents spilled their contents on the flagstones. There were jewels in profusion, torn from the drowned; pearls from the Dirian Sea, amber buckles from Dorak, lapis ear-rings from Tryfarn; the brooches, necklaces and rings of long-dead Queens and Princes. Yet mingled with the precious treasures were tawdry, worthless things: pieces of driftwood, a battered shield, fragments of pottery, cracked shells and dried sponges.

Ellandellore seemed to forget Kerish and, chanting "I am rich. I am rich." he wandered among his treasure, stooping here and there to stroke a statue, blow on a flute or try on a crown.

After a while Kerish said carefully:

"I see that your Majesty is indeed the richest sovereign." He bowed low.

Ellandellore laughed delightedly.

"Look at this crown. I wear it on rainy days."

He held up a silver circlet set with the pale gems known as the Tears of Imarko and made centuries before by a Galkian craftsman for a Prince of Gannoth.

"Oh, and do you like this?"

He handed Kerish a ball of smooth, green stone inlaid

with flaming jewels.

The sorcerer darted across the room to find more favourite treasures to show to his guest, and suddenly pounced on a crude, wooden monkey, once the treasured toy of some Jenozan child.

"This is Illixa, isn't she lovely?"

He hugged the monkey to his breast and crooned over her. Kerish saw then why Elmandis had spoken of the Sorcerer of Tir-Racneth with compassion.

"I am amazed," he repeated. "Even the Emperor of Galkis would envy you such a treasury."

"Yes, but I must have more treasure because I get tired of things."

"Then you should throw away the things you are tired of. That will show how great and rich you are."

"You are right," said Ellandellore. "I like you. What was your name?"

"Kerish-lo-Taan. Shall we be friends?"

"Yes, if you want, and I will throw things away. Here, you can have these."

He tossed the Prince a rope of black pearls. Kerish bowed but refused to take them.

"I thank you, my Emperor, but all I seek is one gold casket. I need it for . . . a game that must be played."

"What kind of game? Can I join in?"

"I will tell you if you give me the casket."

Ellandellore considered this.

"I don't think I can give it to you, but I will show it to you if I can find it. Shall we look?"

The Prince and the sorcerer burrowed through piles of treasure as if they were heaps of rubbish, tossing aside pectorals and chalices, tapestries and manuscripts in their search.

"Found it, found it, I've beaten you!" cried Ellandellore, and from under a fur cloak he drew out a small, golden casket.

"But it's locked and even I can't open it. I've tried everything."

Kerish reached for the casket and suddenly snatched back his hand with a gasp of pain.

"I made it burn you," said Ellandellore calmly. "Your face does look funny. Why are you twisting your mouth like that?"

"Ellandellore," whispered Kerish, "don't you understand pain?"

The sorcerer frowned.

"I remember the word but I don't understand it."

"Then I pity you indeed," said Kerish, cradling his burned hand.

Ellandellore stared at the Prince and began to whimper: "I don't understand. It isn't my fault!"

"Stop it, Ellandellore," snapped Kerish, feeling that it was he who was hundreds of years old not the sorcerer. "You could be taught to understand. Elmandis would help you."

"No he won't, he's angry with me. He told me once he wished I was dead. I remember what that means."

"Ellandellore, I promise you Elmandis would never hurt you," said Kerish, hoping it was true. "He will help you, and if you give me that casket you need never be lonely or frightened again."

The sorcerer stared at him, wide-eyed, for a moment and then giggled:

"No, you shan't have it. I want it for myself."

Fighting a useless desire to do something violent Kerish said reasonably:

"But you have many things more beautiful, great Emperor."

"Yes, but I'm tired of them. I don't know what's inside the casket, so it's not so dull as the other things. Have you brought me anything new?"

Kerish thought frantically. The golden key at his waist must be kept at all costs. There was Kelinda's ring, but he did not want to part with his only remembrance of the Princess of Seld.

While Kerish was thinking Ellandellore sidled up to him and stroked the soft leather of his tunic.

"Nice," he murmured, "the colour of the sea in summer."

He felt a hard lump beneath the cloth and suddenly tugged out the Jewel of Zeldin.

"Oh, beautiful!"

The jewel lit every line of the sorcerer's wondering face.

"But the frozen fire hurts my eyes."

He wrenched at the chain.

"Give it to me!"

"No. It is a jewel of great power and would destroy anyone to whom it was given unwillingly."

Ellandellore believed this sudden invention and drew back.

"I will buy it then. I will give you a crown set with stars. I will give you a sword that can cleave through rock. I will give you a flask of Heartsmead; one drop and the proudest lady in the world will love you. I will give you more treasure than the Godborn hoard in Hildimarn!"

Kerish shook his head.

Ellandellore looked hungrily at the Jewel of Zeldin.

"I will give you the golden casket."

"No."

Kerish's answer was immediate but even as he spoke he thought himself stupid. Surely it was a fair exchange and Izeldon might have meant his gift for just such an occasion. Yet somehow Kerish knew that it would be wrong to part with the jewel before he had even learned what it was or what it could do.

"No," he said unhappily.

"Kerish, will you play a game with me," asked Ellandellore softly, "an easy game, and if you win you shall have the casket and keep your jewel. If I win..." he smiled mischievously, "I keep the casket and the jewel. Will you play, will you?"

"Emperor, how do I know that you will keep your word?"

Ellandellore considered this.

"We could swear a promise if you like."

"Swear by your own power and on pain of your brother's deadly anger," said Kerish sternly.

Ellandellore's face changed.

"Oh but he can't come here, can he?"

"Not unless I let him. He will be able to if you break your word."

"I think you're lying," said Ellandellore fiercely.

"The Godborn do not lie," answered Kerish haughtily. "What is your game?"

"I will take you to the edge of the island," said Ellandellore. "You close your eyes and count to three hundred. Then you turn round. All you have to do is find your way back to Tir-Racneth, and know me and say my name. I swear by my power and my brother's anger to give you the casket if you win, but you have only one guess."

"And if I lose, you have the jewel."

"Yes and..." Ellandellore giggled again, "wait and see."

"Father," thought Kerish, "I will need your gifts now."

Chapter 11

The Book of the Emperors: *Warnings*
*Knowledge without wisdom is like a sharp sword in the
hand of a young child.*

WHEN the *Zeloka* anchored in Rindiss Bay, Elmandis
and Forollkin went ashore and were entertained in
the largest house in the settlement. As Elmandis sat on a
cool terrace overlooking the bay, sipping wine, and
discussing local affairs, Forollkin paced up and down, his
feet scuffing the stones.

"How is your other guest?" Elmandis asked the master
of the house.

"Master Gidjabolgo? I hardly know since he keeps to his
room like a snake under a stone. When he does speak it is to
mock our ways."

"Forgive me for burdening you with him, but he is soon
to travel north with Forollkin."

The host bowed.

"You have my sympathies, Forollkin. Shall I send him
out to you?"

"Well?" asked Elmandis. "Would you like to meet your
new travelling companion?"

"Lord King," Forollkin was almost shouting, "how can
you expect me to care what tricks you are going to play on
us; how can you sit here so calmly while Kerish..."

"Gandalous, my friend," the sorcerer spoke loudly but
placidly, "would you be kind enough to leave us alone for
a time?"

Gandalous gave Forollkin a shocked stare and left the
terrace.

"And by what right did you stop me going with my

brother. . . ? We are not your subjects, we are not your pampered slaves."

A spasm of anger distorted Elmandis' face.

"Forollkin, remember to whom you speak."

"I speak to the King of a strange country. I am told you are a sorcerer, centuries old, and I will try to believe it . . ."

"I could spin out your life through centuries of pain to make you believe it."

"You may threaten till the seas boil," shouted Forollkin, "but I will speak my thoughts. I, at least, am free."

Elmandis raised his hands and opened his lips to speak. In spite of his brave words Forollkin felt fear stab through his stomach. The deadly enchantment welled up from the dark pit of Elmandis' anger, but suddenly the sorcerer broke off, burying his face in his hands.

After a long silence Forollkin knelt by the King's chair and murmured:

"My Lord?"

Elmandis looked up, his eyes as green as the icebergs of the northern ocean, and his voice as cold.

"I will spare you the death that would ease my grief. Come with me to the top of that hill. It overlooks the Straits of Rac."

The two men left the house together and walked up the gentle, green slope. The grass grew lushly there, mingled with scented flowers, and birds sang, unseen, in the trees. On the summit of the hill Elmandis paused and gazed out across the straits to the mists of Cheransee.

"Do not imagine that my inner thoughts have left your brother. Kerish has come to no harm. For a moment there was great danger, but not from Ellandellore."

Elmandis' eyes were open but they were not focused on anything that Forollkin could see.

"He has met the sorcerer and handles him well. Your brother has a cunning tongue but one cannot reason with Ellandellore."

"You will help him though . . ." began Forollkin.

"I cannot while he remains in the territory of Ellandellore, and I would not even if I could," answered the King.

"To win the game he now plays would be a great victory and one he would not wish to share."

"I was not aware that our quest for the keys was a game," said Forollkin indignantly. "I would have thought that you, of all men, would help for your country's sake, and not endanger the quest by pandering to Kerish's pride."

Disconcertingly, Elmandis laughed.

"Forollkin, if anyone endangers this quest, it is you. I know something now of your brother's heart and let me warn you. He loves you but it is a love delicately streaked with hate. If you continue to treat him like a child, he will try to prove to you, by cunning or violence, that he is a child no longer. You know his temper, it is blazoned across your cheek."

"That was just a moment's anger."

"A moment may kill."

"My Lord," said Forollkin firmly, "I swore to the Emperor and the High Priest to protect my brother and I will. I love him and . . ."

"Do you, Forollkin?"

Elmandis turned his cold gaze on the young captain.

"Do you? Is it not rather pleasant to keep a Prince of the Godborn in subjection? Does the son of a concubine not enjoy giving orders to the son of a Queen? You mock the powers of the Godborn because you cannot understand them, yet what would you give to be the Prince . . ."

"No!"

All too clearly Forollkin remembered the hours he had spent listening to his mother's tirades against the Godborn. How often she had complained of the injustice of her strong, brave Forollkin being forced always to take second place to the Prince she hated. He had never heeded her, never consciously envied Kerish or made him suffer for it, never consciously . . .

"Think about it, Forollkin," said Elmandis softly, "while I watch over your brother. There is nothing you can do to help him."

Kerish knew that he was standing on the very edge of a cliff. One step backwards and he would fall two hundred feet on to the jagged rocks below. In front of him was a gentle slope patched with purple flowers and about a mile away, just visible above the hilltops, was the blue tower of Tir-Racneth. This was the picture that Kerish had fixed in his mind before the sorcerer had ordered him to close his eyes and count.

It was a strange experience for Kerish. He had never joined in the games that Galkian children played. Only in the Emperor's garden could he escape from his grave tutors and play as he wanted to; but always alone. He wondered if it might have been the same for Ellandellore and knew that he must win the second key to give the sorcerer of Tir-Racneth a chance to grow up at last.

While he thought, Kerish had been counting automatically. He reached three hundred, stopped and opened his eyes. He was standing again in the waste of grey sand with black shapes savaging the distance. Cautiously Kerish inched one heel backwards. As he had expected, what looked like sand was space. If he stepped back he would fall to his death.

Wondering how many players of Ellandellore's games had taken that fatal step, Kerish walked slowly forward. In his mind he held firmly to the memory of the grassy hills of Cheransee. He knew he could not trust his eyes, and he was unsure whether what he heard and smelt was true or false. In both reality and illusion, the sea dominated.

Kerish closed his eyes again and went forward like a blind man, stretching out his hands to feel for obstacles. After a few minutes of this he kicked off his boots and, to his relief, felt the grass beneath his bare feet. Slowly but confidently he moved towards Tir-Racneth.

Suddenly above the muted thunder of the sea sounded a terrible scream, a sound that no human mouth could have formed. Kerish's whole body was jolted with the shock of it and, without thinking, he opened his eyes. It was the worst mistake he could have made. The image of the gentle hills was stripped from his mind and he was back among the screaming rocks. Like spears thrown by the earth to skewer the sun, the rocks thrust upward, fragmenting the light.

Caged in stone Kerish closed his eyes again and ran forward. His hands met jagged rock and he flinched back. Opening his eyes he saw blood trickling down his fingers. If he was bleeding the rocks must be real...

Kerish tried desperately to force his thoughts into calm disbelief. With the end of his sash he wiped away the blood. There were no cuts beneath.

Kerish tried to replace the confidence he had lost by rebuilding the picture of the true way ahead, but even in his mind's eye the black rock tore through the grassy slopes and the blue tower dissolved into the mist. He knew the rocks would trap him until he had the trust to walk through their seeming solidity. He stood quite still and thought instead of something easier to visualize — the Emperor's garden. Just as the remembered groves and pools and pavilions began to soothe him, the scream sounded again.

Kerish shouted, trying to drown the sound with a jumble of meaningless phrases. Attuned with horrible accuracy to the dark places of his memory, the sound coalesced into a long-suppressed nightmare. The scream sounded for a third time, filled with the fierce joy of a creature sighting its helpless prey.

Catching Kerish's thoughts Ellandellore moulded them into a substance. Something began to move close by, dragging its gorged body across the rocks. Kerish could hear the rasping of its scales and claws. He shut his eyes but the screaming rocks seemed etched on his lids. There was no escape from the rocks or from the creature that crawled over them. It reared above him, blocking out the last of the sunlight. Retching at its foul stench he reeled back against the rocks and waited, paralysed, for death.

As the black coils slid towards him Kerish clutched the Jewel of Zeldin and wondered distantly if he would die torn by the terrible claws or crushed in the huge mouth. The thought was so horrible that it was no longer quite believable. Though the claws would reach him in a few seconds Kerish could not imagine so horrible a death.

It was as if he had already passed over the chasm of death and could watch his threatened body from the other side with complete indifference. The rocks at his back no longer seemed the bars of a cage, but like strong arms supporting him, holding him safe and steady. Their strength seemed to flow into him and he remembered the touch of his father's hands.

"Beloved son, I give you courage."

Kerish heard the words and he was not afraid.

The Prince of the Godborn opened his eyes and found himself standing on a quiet grey-green hillside. He stood there for a long time, completely forgetting the game until a gust of wind tugged at the chain around his waist and slapped the golden key against his thigh. Then he hurried towards Tir-Racneth and Ellandellore could draw on his thoughts to attack him again.

The sorcerer conjured images of the dying Gankali to stagger towards Kerish imploring his aid. He barred the path with an alabaster sarcophagus, whose lid was cracking open, and with Brigands of Fangmere, whirling axes. To Kerish they seemed as remote as illustrations to some work of ancient history. He paced steadily towards them and they dissolved away. Desperately Ellandellore tried to impose the Emperor's garden with its vividly-remembered dangers, but through its hazy image Kerish still saw the landscape of Cheransee. With each firm step he ripped the veil of illusion. Ellandellore flung vision after vision at the rock of the Prince's calm. Kerish scarcely noticed them.

He climbed the last hill and pushed open the door of the blue tower. Inside, among the glittering debris, his confidence slowly ebbed away. He felt as though he were shedding a suit of heavy armour, piece by piece. He was almost glad to be rid of the weight, but it left him exposed again.

No living thing moved among the dusty treasures. The gilded shackles of the dead were there in profusion, but no Ellandellore. Kerish understood now what the sorcerer had meant by saying, "Find me and know me."

"Imarko, aid me," he thought gloomily; "how can I possibly recognize him? There are thousands of things in this room. He might have taken the form of any one of them."

Kerish checked himself.

"I am my father's son. I must use the sight of the Godborn."

He took a deep breath, folded his hands over the jewel at his breast and looked round the room. It seemed to him infinitely pathetic.

Kerish tried to imagine himself inside the mind of the child sorcerer. Where would he choose to hide? What would he be? A queen's crown? A noose of pearls? A wave-worn pebble? None of these surely.

Sighing, Kerish stooped to pick up the battered wooden monkey that lay at his feet. The poor toy that Ellandellore loved, the broken ... no, this was not broken. The toy was quite whole.

"Ellandellore," whispered Kerish, and found himself holding the sorcerer by the shoulders, "I know you; the game is mine."

"I suppose so," Ellandellore pouted, "but I did frighten you, didn't I?"

"A great deal," admitted Kerish. "Now give me my prize."

"I don't want to," said the sorcerer sulkily.

"You must," answered Kerish calmly, "or there can be no more games."

"All right then."

Smiling again the sorcerer scrabbled through a heap of uncut gems and brought out the golden casket.

Kerish took out Elmandis' key and unlocked the casket. Inside lay a second key set with a pale azure gem. Kerish hung both keys on the chain about his waist.

"You have two pretty keys and I haven't any," said Ellandellore jealously. "It isn't fair."

"But look at all the other things you have!"

Kerish gestured at the glittering heaps of treasure.

"I hate them!" wailed Ellandellore and his green eyes brimmed with tears. "I want you to stay and play with me."

"You promised to let me go."

"No I didn't, I only promised to give you the casket. I won't stay here alone any more. I'm frightened."

"Come back with me to Ellerinonn," said Kerish

gently. "Elmandis would be glad to see you and they are kind people there."

"No, Elmandis would punish me. I won't go!" He sounded genuinely terrified. "We'll stay here."

"All right, Ellandellore," said Kerish wearily, "I'll stay and we will play another game."

The sorcerer looked up, his eyes bright with tears.

"What sort of game?"

"I'll hide and you can come and look for me."

"Yes. Where will you hide?"

"That's my secret. Now close your eyes and count to a thousand. When you've finished you can come looking."

Obediently Ellandellore began to count.

As Kerish slipped out of the treasure chamber he glanced for the last time at the sorcerer of Tir-Racneth, a small figure in gaudy rags, a crooked crown on his head and tears still trailing down his cheeks.

As the Prince fled light-footed down the hill he reasoned with his conscience. He had no choice but to trick Ellandellore for the sake of the keys.

"And how many other lies will you have to tell before this quest is over?" Kerish asked himself. "At least I'm not harming Ellandellore; surely now Elmandis will help his brother? But to leave a child crying ... He is no child; think of all those shapes, the men he has murdered. Can a child murder?"

Kerish's thoughts were jolted back to the present. If Ellandellore discovered that his visitor was running away he would be dangerous. Kerish found a narrow path that he hoped led down to the sea. He slithered down it, hurting his bare feet on rock and shingle, till he reached the cool sand. For a moment he flared up in panic. The sea lay in front of him but there was no boat waiting at the tide's edge. Then he saw it, a black speck in the distance, perhaps half a mile along the beach. The twisting path had brought him too far east.

Kerish ran. It was not easy, for his feet kept sinking into the soft sand, but at last, fighting for breath, Kerish flung himself at the boat and pushed it out to sea.

When the water was up to his knees he heaved himself

in. He lay exhausted for a moment and then pressed his lips to the timbers and whispered the words Elmandis had taught him and the name of Rindiss Bay. A shudder passed through the boat as if it were still a black tree, bowing to the wind in the mountains of Gol. Then it slid slowly forward, breasting the white waves to reach the calm purple of the deep waters.

As the shores of Cheransee grew fainter a mood of exultation crept over Kerish. He had won two keys with no help from Forollkin!

A distant shriek of anger and distress aroused him. Looking back he saw the small, bright-haired figure of Ellandellore standing on a cliff-top. Instinctively Kerish shrank down but the mists swallowed the childish form and surely he was out of the sorcerer's power.

The black boat sped skilfully on, faster and faster. The coast of Ellerinonn was in sight.

Kerish shut out the thought that the craft his life depended on belonged to the angry sorcerer. He had a destiny. Zeldin would not let him die. He concentrated on happy memories, a trip to Trykis with Forollkin, afternoons spent with Kelinda reading favourite poems; but all the time he was listening for the first fatal crunch as the boat dashed itself against some jagged rock. It did not come, for Ellandellore knew that it was crueller to let his victims think they had escaped.

When the boat was barely a mile from the coast of Ellerinonn and safety, Kerish sat up and stretched. As if in answer, a gust of wind jolted the boat and Kerish fell back, banging his head. He struggled to sit up again and saw that the sky was turning black. The wind screamed like the rocks of Cheransee and lashed the waves into a fury. Ellandellore had sent a storm to drown the golden keys.

Kerish, his hair whipping at his white face, watched in horror as a towering wave swept towards him. The boat was still moving towards Ellerinonn but it would never reach the shore.

A huge wall of water hit the black craft and overturned it. Kerish was thrown into the sea. He remembered somehow to shut his mouth and stopped swallowing seawater. He clawed his way to the surface but was pressed down again by a second wave. In a dark inferno Kerish struggled wildly to reach the air before the pain in his chest became unbearable. For a brief moment he surfaced, gulped down air and water and sank again.

While his body fought for life, his thoughts were like a whirlpool of disconnected images. The blue and golden ceiling of his bedroom in Galkis, the stupid expression on Forollkin's face as the whip lashed his cheek, Li-Kroch clutching a child who was not his son, the Emperor orchid almost in flower, the zeloka flying through his dreams. They vanished almost before he recognized them but just before the darkness swallowed him Kerish seemed to see the tearful face of Ellandellore and to hear Elmandis calling him home.

It was light, so it must be day, Kerish told himself drowsily.

"Have I slept late?"

Slowly a room seemed to materialize around him and Kerish realized that he was lying in bed staring up at the ceiling. With what felt like a very great effort, he turned his head and found himself staring at someone whose presence was reassuring.

"Kerish? Are you awake?"

Forollkin leaned over his brother.

"Really awake?"

"I think so," whispered the Prince.

"You must know whether you are awake or not," snapped Forollkin, suddenly and unreasonably angry.

His brother's great purple, black and golden eyes gazed up at him blankly.

"Kerish?"

Hearing their voices, Elmandis entered from the next room carrying a crystal cup, filled with some clear liquid. Crossing to the bed he held the cup to Kerish's lips and Forollkin slipped his hand under his brother's head to support him. Kerish drank and the fiery liquid seared away the mists from his mind and jerked him awake.

He pushed the cup away.

"It tastes terrible. I don't want any more."

"He is himself again," said Elmandis lightly.

"Imarko be praised," muttered Forollkin, his thoughts dragging him back to the sight of Elmandis sucking the fury of the storm into himself, tossing back the tide with a flick of his hand and lifting Kerish from the suddenly exposed sea-bed.

Though the storm still raged in the sorcerer's eyes Forollkin had been afraid that nothing could save Kerish. He could have sworn that his brother's breathing had already stopped but Elmandis had sent him out of the room and when he returned Kerish was sleeping peacefully.

Dizzily, the Prince was trying to sit up but Elmandis pushed him gently back against the pillows.

"No, Kerish, you must rest, for your body has not yet caught up with your mind's strength and tomorrow you must begin your journey again."

"But the keys!" persisted Kerish. "Did I lose them in the storm?"

"No," said Elmandis shortly.

Kerish delved under the sheet and found the golden chain still knotted round his waist.

"I did it then, I really did it?"

Forollkin cleared his throat and said, a little stiffly: "I am proud of you, Kerish."

The Prince gave his brother an affectionate hug and looked up eagerly to Elmandis.

"My Lord, what must we do next? Where must we go?"

"I have already told Captain Engis that you will be sailing to Pin-Drouth," answered Elmandis.

"Pin-Drouth, the Frian capital!" exclaimed Forollkin. "But there is nothing in Lan-Pin-Fria but swamps."

"True enough, and I hope you will enjoy your journey through them."

"But where are we going?" demanded Kerish.

"Tomorrow you will know. Tonight you rest," said Elmandis implacably, and left them together.

After Kerish had picked at a light supper Forollkin insisted that he try to sleep again. Kerish huddled down beneath the sheets but he did not sleep. His mind went relentlessly over and over the events of the past months.

He heard Ka-Metranee's curse, the despair in his father's voice and the screams of the dying on the *Zeloka*'s embattled deck. He could not shake off the images of Yxin's sneering face, the Emperor crouched over an alabaster sarcophagus, Zyrindella cowering before Zeldin's statue and Ellandellore weeping.

Just after midnight Elmandis came quietly into the room carrying a lamp.

"Kerish, are you troubled?"

"I can't sleep. I just keep thinking about things that have happened."

"I cannot free you from the spectres of the past. Be grateful you have only eighteen years of them, but I will fetch you a sleeping draught."

"My Lord, what will happen to Ellandellore?" asked Kerish.

Elmandis looked down at the lamp he held and said, without expression:

"He tried to kill you."

"I tricked him. I abandoned him, and he was so alone!"

Elmandis put down the lamp and his face was in darkness.

"You are more gentle with us than we deserve."

"What will happen to him?" repeated Kerish.

"Without the key he will begin to age. His awakening from childhood will be a painful one," answered Elmandis.

"You won't leave him alone there?"

"Even without our keys most of our power will remain for our natural lives. I can ask him to come to me but I cannot force him," said the Lord of Tir-Racneth's brother.

"I think he will come, if you keep asking."

"You must have guessed, Kerish, that it was I who made him what he is. If I had not both spoiled and neglected him . . ."

"My Lord, that is far in the past." Kerish reached out to Elmandis but the sorcerer flinched back.

"Now that you have our keys, I suppose it is. My mistakes will no longer seem as black as the day they were made. I will fetch you your draught, Kerish."

When the sorcerer brought him a cup of indigo liquid Kerish drank gratefully, slept for eight hours and woke ravenously hungry. He was in the middle of a large breakfast when Forollkin stalked in. The young captain sat down with a thump on the bed, spilling a jug of milk all over the sheets. When that had been cleared up Kerish asked what was the matter. He could not recall having done anything recently to annoy his brother.

"Oh, it isn't you, Kerish."

"What then? You look as if you've been stung by an irk-fly."

"So I have, though one without wings."

"You're speaking in riddles. What do you mean?"

Forollkin replied with uncharacteristic sarcasm: "I have had the honour and pleasure of meeting our travelling companion, Master Gidjabolgo."

"Oh well, Elmandis did say . . ." began Kerish.

"Yes, Elmandis. I shall have a few choice words to say to him when next we meet."

"Then by all means say them now," murmured the King of Ellerinonn, who had come quietly into the room. Kerish grinned as Forollkin shrank under the cool gaze and muttered an apology.

Elmandis laughed. "You will never master Gidjabolgo if you are so easily put down. Look on him as a challenge. He will at least enliven your journey through Lan-Pin-Fria."

"My Lord, you promised . . ."

"To tell you where you are going? Yes, Forollkin."

Elmandis sat down in a tall chair by the bed.

"You are going north to the Ultimate Mountains, to the edge of the world. You look startled, Forollkin."

"But there is nothing there, just ice and snow and mountain after mountain, by all I ever heard."

"There is the Citadel of Tir-Zulmar and its solitary sorcerer."

"How shall we reach it?" asked Kerish.

"Since you must journey the length of Lan-Pin-Fria, I would suggest that you buy yourselves a passage on a Frian boat sailing north. It would be wisest to travel as minor Galkian noblemen. I see from your impatient look, Forollkin, that you've already been given that advice; obey it then. Lan-Pin-Fria is a land of rivers and you must follow the greatest of them to its source. Let the waters of the Pin-Fran be your only guide."

Elmandis looked from the Prince's eager eyes to Forollkin's anxious frown. "Follow the river," he repeated, "when all other guides fail. Follow it beyond the last town and village, beyond the Forbidden Hill, beyond mountain after mountain, to the edge of Zindar. Only then will you find Tir-Zulmar."

Kerish found that he was already shivering as if the Enchanter King breathed out the cold of the Ultimate Mountains, but Forollkin said brusquely: "Can you tell us something about this mountain sorcerer?"

"I could," replied Elmandis, "but I will not. I have fulfilled the terms of Zeldin's bargain; he can ask no more of me."

"I'm sure that you have done more for us than Zeldin asked of you," declared Kerish.

Elmandis stood up. "Prince," he said curtly, "your ship sails with the noon tide."

Kerish got out of bed and dressed, feeling weaker than he cared to admit. Very slowly, he and Forollkin walked down towards the beach. It was a glorious morning. The sunlight splintered on the dazzling white of Ellerinionn marble. Flowers defied the noonday heat and on the beach children were being taught to write, drawing characters in the sand.

A small boat was waiting in the shallows to take them out to the *Zeloka*. Elmandis stood close by, the waves breaking over his feet. He watched Forollkin leap into the boat and merely said, "Remember what I said to you here." He kissed Kerish on the forehead and for the first time the Prince noticed strands of grey in the flaxen hair.

"Will I meet you again?"

"Not in Ellerinonn," answered Elmandis.

Reluctantly Kerish stepped into the boat. Two men from the *Zeloka* pushed it out, climbed in and began to row. Elmandis waded after them till the water was above his waist. Kerish looked back until he was forced to concentrate on climbing the swinging ladder to the *Zeloka*'s deck. When he reached the top and turned towards the shore again, Elmandis had gone.

The Prince became slowly aware that Captain Engis was welcoming him aboard and saying something about finding room in the crew's quarters for Gidjabolgo.

"Gidjabolgo?"

"He came aboard last night, your Highness. I didn't quite know . . ."

"His Highness is tired," said Forollkin brusquely. "Talk to me about it later."

Kerish found himself being led to his cabin and forced to lie down. While Forollkin fussed over him, talking of potions and keeping warm, and resting, depression crept over Kerish. He was glad he did not have to watch the coast of Ellerinonn as it receded but nor did he want to lie in his cabin with no company but his own dreary thoughts.

"I brought some inks and parchment with me for drawing; do you think you could find them?"

Surprisingly, Forollkin did not argue, and Kerish was soon propped up in bed meticulously copying a text from the Book of Sorrows and framing it with garlands of interwoven flowers and birds.

The *Zeloka* sailed north. She would call first at For-Lessel to bring the news of Gankali's death to her father, and then at Pin-Drouth, capital and chief port of the Land of Four Rivers. For three days Kerish kept to his cabin, quietly absorbed in the texts he illuminated, but on the fourth evening he came on deck to share a meal with Forollkin and Engis.

Wrapped in a fur cloak against the sea breezes, Kerish sat eating kardiss from a porcelain bowl and drinking the hot, spiced wine, beloved of Galkian travellers.

"What light is that?" asked Forollkin suddenly.

"Where?"

Forollkin pointed but the Prince could see nothing.

"It's gone now," admitted his brother. "We must be a long way from land; perhaps it was a ship . . . wait, there it is again."

In the distance a blue light flared.

"My Lords." Engis strode over to his passengers. "My Lords, don't look. Turn your faces away."

"Why, Captain? Surely a light can do no harm?"

"Not to your Highness perhaps, but I have known men turned mad by the light of that blue flame. Mad enough to leap overboard and drown trying to reach it."

"Where does the light come from?"

"From the rocks of Lind, Lord Forollkin."

"I have heard of them," said Kerish, "and I think they have an evil name."

"True, your Highness," muttered Engis. "The rocks form a circle and for miles around them the sea is shallow and treacherous. Many ships have been lost there. Yet what causes the light no one knows. Some say that within the rocks lies a small island and that poor souls washed ashore from the wrecks light fires to signal for help; but what ship could rescue them from there? Others say that blue demons live among the rocks and delight in luring ships to their doom. I don't know, and this is the nearest I ever sail to Lind."

"Gallant Captain, are you then afraid of fanciful tales, told to frighten children? Shame on you, you've made Lord Forollkin tremble like an arrow just struck."

Engis swore under his breath.

Forollkin stood up and Kerish twisted round to discover the owner of the rasping voice.

A man, short and broad, stood in the dimness about the hatchway. Kerish could not see him properly until the stranger moved forward into the torchlight. Then Gidja-bolgo the Forgite and Prince Kerish-lo-Taan stared at each other, both equally startled.

Kerish had never in all his life seen anyone so ugly. Colourless eyes bulged in the Forgite's moon-face while a crooked nose squatted flatly between. Thin lips were twisted back to show broken teeth and a tongue too big for the mouth, and the dome of his huge head was barely covered by wisps of reddish hair. The body was as mis-shapen as the head, with arms that were far too long and

180

hands that looked as plump and clumsy as a baby's. There was nothing frightening or sinister about Gidjabolgo's ugliness; he missed even that dignity. The Forgite was merely ridiculous and helpless; unforgivably, Kerish threw back his head and laughed.

After a moment Gidjabolgo answered with a sneer: "So this is the sickly Princeling who can't stand a ducking without taking to his bed like a woman in labour?"

There was an appalled silence.

To a loyal Galkian, Gidjabolgo's words were not merely insulting but verging on sacrilege. Even so, Kerish tried to control the anger surging through him.

"Perhaps you have never been near to drowning, and that is why you speak of it so lightly. It is an experience you may try if you let your tongue run away with your wits again in my presence."

Gidjabolgo bowed with a derisive flourish.

"I see your Highness rules by tyranny and a poor Forgite can be drowned at your whim."

"This is a Galkian ship and all aboard it are subject to Galkian law," said Kerish. "I will spare you the penalty for insolence to the Godborn, since I take it that you are ignorant of civilized manners."

The Forgite's face contorted into a fiercer ugliness.

"I see no gods here, only a spoilt child prattling threats in imitation of his elders."

"Throw him over the side," said Kerish calmly.

After a moment men moved to obey, but Forollkin sprang forward to stop them.

"Highness, you promised to take him with us!"

Trembling with anger, Kerish said nothing and three of Engis' crew dragged Gidjabolgo towards the rail. As they reached it the Forgite began to shriek.

"Kerish, order them to stop!" shouted Forollkin.

The Prince's face was blank. He stared through Forollkin as if he no longer acknowledged his brother's existence but at the last possible moment he called:

"Stop. Bring him here to me."

The sailors tossed Gidjabolgo down at their Prince's feet.

"I have brought you to the edge of death to teach you courtesy. Take him below and be sure to keep him out of my sight."

"I am privileged to have witnessed the famous justice of the Godborn," hissed Gidjabolgo as they dragged him away. "Ever merciful to their victims, ever . . ."

The rest of the speech was cut off by the slamming of the hatch.

His anger ebbing, Kerish was already ashamed of himself. Forollkin gazed warily at his brother, wondering if he had, even for a moment, intended to see the Forgite drowned. No. Forollkin tried to dismiss the thought and the echo of Elmandis' words: "With cunning or violence . . ."

What had possessed the man to provoke the Prince so? Kerish was uncomfortably conscious of the stares of Engis and his crew. Perhaps they were wondering why a Prince of the Godborn could not strike the Forgite dumb.

"What faith will they have left in the Godborn," thought Kerish bitterly, "when this voyage is over?"

"Highness." It was Forollkin's voice. "You look very tired. Perhaps you should go to your cabin."

For the rest of the voyage Kerish-lo-Taan rarely emerged from his quarters.

At For-Lessel Forollkin went ashore with Captain Engis to visit Gankali's father. The Merchant Prince received the news of his daughter's death with little emotion. The only distress he showed was at the prospect of lengthy negotiations on the return of her dowry.

Afterwards Forollkin spent a long time in the market square at the heart of the city, choosing and haggling over a belated birthday present for Kerish.

Gidjabolgo showed no inclination to emerge from the bowels of the ship to visit his home and the *Zeloka* sailed after only twelve hours in port. Three days later they sighted the coast of Lan-Pin-Fria.

Pin-Drouth was built on a marshy island in the middle of a delta. For most of the year the river rolled sluggishly around the island but in the rainy season it flooded the city so all its wooden buildings had to be raised on stilts. In autumn the streets were free of water but coated with dried mud and slime that bred disease and the Galkians came on deck to face a moist, suffocating heat.

Already the *Zeloka* was besieged by pedlars proffering paper fans, cheap sandals, gilt trinkets, amulets, dried ob-fish and other Frian delicacies.

There were beggars too, some horribly mutilated or deformed. Appalled, Kerish wanted to distribute alms at once but Engis asked him not to be too generous . . . "Or we shall have every beggar in the city on this quay, with thieves in their wake eager to fleece a stranger."

A purse was brought and several of the *Zeloka's* crew went down among the beggars to see that the money was divided equally. Even so scuffles broke out and the blind and the lame scrabbled in the dust for fallen coins.

Trying to distract his passengers from the ugly sight, Engis pointed out some of the Frian castes from among the crowd on the quay.

There were shaven-headed serfs, their thin, brown bodies beaded with sweat. The free artisans, distinguished by their short hair and copper bracelets, looked scarcely happier or more prosperous. Both these castes bowed obsequiously when a Merchant or a Hunter passed. The Merchants were grey-skinned with distinctive moss-green hair. They wore ankle-length pleated kilts and a fortune in bracelets, collars and ear-rings of green bronze. Most of them looked too fat to walk and were carried in wicker chairs by their panting serfs.

Forollkin watched them with contempt, but his expression changed when Engis pointed to a Hunter.

"That is a killer of Or-gar-gees."

"Of what?"

"An Or-gar-gee is a water serpent," explained Engis. "They grow huge in the northern marshes and their skins are highly prized."

The Hunter was tall and lean. He wore only a brief linen kilt and boots and a wide collar of some scaled skin. His shaven head was crowned by a knot of green hair passed through a ring of bronze and long, curved teeth dangled from his ears. The Hunter held a slender spear and strode proudly through the crowd without acknowledging their greetings.

A jingling noise drew the Galkians' attention to an old man pushing his way through a group of serfs. Hundreds of bronze rings were fastened to his tattered clothing and they clashed together as he moved. His hair hung loose to his waist and his face was garishly painted. The old man lifted up a crude, wooden idol and began yelling at the top of his voice to extol the virtues of his god.

"The Frians have more gods than there are reeds in the marshes," said Engis with disgust. "That is one of their holy men, promising to cure all the ills of life for a mere three rings of bronze. This is a savage place. Still, my Lords, there are some merchants who have travelled and learned a little of our ways. I'll visit those I know and try to arrange a passage north for you."

When Engis had gone the brothers did not linger on deck. The beggars were already shouting again for alms.

"How long will our journey through Fria take?" asked Kerish.

"Months," said Forollkin gloomily.

Engis returned with the news that if they were prepared to leave the next day, the Prince and his brother could travel north on the ship of a merchant named Ibrogdiss.

"I don't like the man," reported Engis, "but he speaks good Zindaric and should honour a bargain sealed with gold."

"He accepted our story?" asked Forollkin.

"Without a flicker. Frians expect all foreigners to be madmen," said Engis, "begging your Lordship's pardon."

It had been Kerish's idea to pose as minor Galkian noblemen collecting specimens from the marshes for the Emperor's garden.

Forollkin went with Engis to his cabin to give him his final orders. The *Zeloka* was to sail to Mel-Selnor, the chief port of Seld, with letters for Queen Pellameera. She would call at Pin-Drouth on her return and on her next outward voyage, to seek news of the Prince.

Engis begged Forollkin to take some Galkian soldiers

with him into the wild Frian interior but he firmly refused. They must travel as inconspicuously as possible, and Gidjabolgo would be their only companion.

Forollkin did not, however, decline a farewell cup of wine. The cup became a flask and the flask a flagon and Engis' tales of seafaring adventures more and more improbable.

In a life hedged by ceremony Forollkin had had few opportunities to get drunk in good company, so he took this chance with a will. The sound of raucous but contented singing soon floated out across the harbour.

As the sudden Frian night descended, Kerish lit a lamp of translucent jade and selected a pile of clothes, jewels and possessions that would fit into the single, light chest that was all Forollkin would allow him to take. There were three things he could not bear to part with: his copy of the Book of the Emperors, the jewelled pieces of his Zel set, and his zildar. That, at least, he could carry slung over his shoulder, so Forollkin could not object. To these he added two gifts: the painted flask from Ellerinonn filled with the Blood of the Sun, and a casket of pale ivory.

Twenty years before, the Emperor of Galkis had ordered his craftsmen to make a necklace of moonflowers from shining cirge and cloudy gems. One spring morning he had placed it in a casket as exquisite as itself and presented both to his beloved Taana. Now the Emperor had given the necklace to Taana's son, for his bride to wear on her wedding day.

Kerish wondered if he could ever love a woman as intensely as his father had loved Taana. Until her death, Ka-Litraan had been a good Emperor and had striven hard against the coming darkness. Kerish thought about his father as he undressed and murmured his evening prayers. He slept almost as soon as he lay down and failed to hear Forollkin's unsteady progress to his cabin, or the sacrilegious comments of the crew.

Both the brothers woke before dawn and dressed by lamplight. The Prince's chest was crammed so full that two soldiers had to sit on the lid before it could be fastened. Kerish looked wistfully back at all the things he was forced to leave behind: though unimportant in themselves, they were reminders of home.

He wrapped his blue cloak around him and quietly closed the cabin door. On deck Forollkin and Gidjabolgo and their meagre luggage were waiting.

Kerish noticed at once how pale Forollkin looked, and asked if he was well. With an embarrassed glance at Engis, Forollkin muttered something about a headache.

Gidjabolgo's unpleasant laugh broke through Kerish's reply:

"My poor master, his brain hasn't dried out yet. It's still clogged with Tryfanian wine. Just as well we're leaving." The Forgite pitched his voice to reach Engis. "Who knows how straight this ship will sail today?"

The captain's face suffused with anger. Kerish hastily repressed a grin and said: "Is everything ready?"

"Yes, your Highness."

Four Galkian soldiers hoisted the luggage on their shoulders to take it half a mile up river to where Ibrogdiss' ship was moored.

Kerish extended his hand to Engis and the captain knelt to kiss it.

"We have much to thank you for, captain," said Kerish. "The Governor of Ephaan told me that you were the best captain in the fleet and I have seen ample proof of it."

"Your Highness, I would ask a favour," murmured Engis.

"Name it."

"My men have asked if you will bless them."

Shocked and humbled by their faith, Kerish quietly agreed. One by one the crew knelt before him and the Prince traced the ancient sign for peace on their foreheads.

Then it was time.

The crew crowded to the rails to watch the Prince and his escort leave. At the bottom of the gangplank both brothers paused to look back at the ship and the great purple and golden wings of her figurehead. This seemed a more final and a far more painful parting than leaving Ephaan.

The *Zeloka* had been part of Galkis but now they would be alone in an alien country.

From now on they had only each other.